Books by Poul Anderson

ENSIGN FLANDRY
THE LONG WAY HOME
THE MAN WHO COUNTS
THE NIGHT FACE
THE PEREGRINE
QUESTION AND ANSWER
WORLD WITHOUT STARS
FLANDRY OF TERRA
AGENT OF THE TERRAN EMPIRE

All from ACE Science Fiction

SF

POUL ANDERSON
A STONE IN HEAVEN

Afterword by Sandra Miesel

SF

ace books

A Division of Charter Communications Inc.
A GROSSET & DUNLAP COMPANY
51 Madison Avenue
New York, New York 10010

An ACE Book

Cover art by Michael Whelan

First Ace printing: October 1979

This edition: June 1980

2 4 6 8 0 9 7 5 3
Manufactured in the United States of America

To John K. Hord

I

Through time beyond knowing, the Kulembarach clan had ranged those lands which reach south of Lake Roah and east of the Kiiong River. The Forebear was said to have brought her family up from the Ringdales while the Ice was still withdrawing beyond the Guardian Mountains. Her descendants were there on the territory she took when traders from West-Oversea brought in the arts of ironworking and writing. They were old in possession when the first Seekers of Wisdom arose, and no few of them joined the College as generations passed. They were many and powerful when the long-slumbering fires in Mount Gungnor awoke again, and the Golden Tide flowed forth to enrich this whole country, and the clans together established the Lords of the Volcano. They were foremost in welcoming and dealing with the strangers from the stars.

But about that time, the Ice began returning, and now the folk of Kulembarach were in as ill a plight as any of their neighbors.

Yewwl had gone on a long hunt with her husband Robreng and their three youngest children, Ngao,

Ych, and little Ungn. That was only partly to get food, when the ranchlands could no more support enough livestock. It was also to get away, move about, unleash some of their rage against the fates upon game animals. Besides, her oath-sister Banner was eager to learn how regions distant from Wainwright Station were changed by cold and snow, and Yewwl was glad to oblige.

The family rode east for an afternoon and most of the following night. Though they did not hurry, and often stopped to give chase or to rest, that much travel took them a great ways, to one of the horn-topped menhirs which marked the territorial border of the Arrohdzaroch clan. Scarcity of meat would have made trespass dangerous as well as wrong. Yewwl turned off in a northwesterly direction.

"We will go home by way of the Shrine," she explained to the others — and to Banner, who saw and heard and even felt what she did, through the collar around her neck. Had she wished to address the human unheard by anybody else, she would have formed the words voicelessly, down in her throat.

The alien tone never came to any hearing but Yewwl's; Banner had said the sound went in through her skull. Eighteen years had taught Yewwl to recognize trouble in it: "I've seen pictures lately, taken from moon-height. You would not like what you found there, dear."

Fur bristled, vanes spread and rippled, in sign of defiance. "I understand that. Shall the Ice keep me from my Forebear?" Anger died out. For Banner alone, Yewwl added softly, "And those with me hope for a token from her — an oracular dream, perhaps. And . . . I may be an unbeliever in such things, because of you, but I myself can nonetheless draw strength from them."

Her band rode on. Night faded into hours of slowly brightening twilight. The storminess common around dawn and sunset did not come. Instead was eerie quiet under a moon and a half. The nullfire hereabouts did not grow tall, as out on the veldt, but formed a thick turf, hoarfrost-white, that muffled the hoofbeats of the onsars. Small crepuscular creatures were abroad, darters, scuttlers, light-flashers, and the chill was softened by a fragrance of nightwort, but life had grown scant since Yewwl and Robreng were young. They felt how silence starkened the desolation, and welcomed a wind that sprang up near morning, though it bit them to the bone and made stands of spearcane rattle like skeletons.

The sun rose at last. For a while it was a red step pyramid, far and far on the blurry horizon. The sky was opalescent. Below, land rolled steeply upward, cresting in a thousand-meter peak where snow and ice flushed in the early light. That burden spilled down the slopes and across the hills, broken here and there by a crag, a boulder, a tawny patch of uncovered nullfire, a tree—brightcrown or sawfrond—which the cold had slain. A flyer hovered aloft, wings dark against a squat mass of clouds. Yewwl didn't recognize its kind. Strange things from beyond the Guardian Range were moving in with the freeze.

Ungn, her infant, stirred and mewed in her pouch. Her belly muscles seemed to glow with it. She might have stopped and dismounted to feed him, but a ruddy canyon and a tarn gone steel-hard told her through memory how near she was to her goal. She jabbed foot-claws at her onsar's extensors and the beast stepped up its pace from a walk to a shamble, as if realizing, weary though it was and rapidly though the air was thinning, that it could soon rest. Yewwl reached into a saddlebag, took forth a strip of dried meat, swallowed a part for herself and chewed the remainder into pulp. Meanwhile she had lifted Ungn into her arms and cuddled him. Her vanes she folded around her front to give the beloved mite shelter from the whining, seeking wind.

Ych rode ahead. The sun entered heaven fully, became round and dazzling, gilded his pelt and sent light aflow over the vanes that he spread in sheer eagerness. He was nearly grown, lithe, handsome; no ruinous weather could dim the pride of his youth. His sister Ngao, his junior by three years, rode behind, leading several pack animals which bore camp gear and the smoked spoils of the hunt. She was slightly built and quiet, but Yewwl knew she was going to become a real beauty. Let fate be kind to her!

Having well masticated the food, the mother brought her lips around her baby's and, with the help of her tongue, fed him. He gurgled and went back to sleep. She imagined him doing it happily, but knew that was mere imagination. Just six days old—or fourteen, if you counted from his begetting—he was as yet tiny and unshapen. His eyes wouldn't open for another four or five days, and he wouldn't be crawling around on his own till almost half a year after that.

Robreng drew alongside. "Here," Yewwl said. "You take him a while." She handed Ungn over for her husband to tuck in his pouch. With a close look: "What's wrong?"

The tautness of his vane-ribs, the quivering along their surfaces, the backward slant of his ears, everything about him cried unease. He need but say: "I sense grief before us."

Yewwl lifted her right thigh to bring within reach the knife sheathed there. (Strapped to the left was a purse for flint, steel, tinderbox, and other such objects.) "Beasts?" Veldt lopers seldom attacked folk,

but a pack of them—or some different kind of carnivore—might have been driven desperate by hunger. "Invaders?" The nightmare which never ended was of being overrun by foreigners whom starvation had forced out of their proper territory.

His muzzle wrinkled, baring fangs, in a negative. "Not those, as far as I can tell. But things feel wrong here."

In twenty years of marriage, she had learned to trust his judgment nearly as much as her own. While a bachelor, he had fared widely around, even spending two seasons north of the Guardians to hunt in the untenanted barrens there. He it was who had argued, when last the clan leaders met before the Lord of the Volcano, that this country need not be abandoned. Orchards and grazing would wither, ranching come to an end, but creatures native to the cold lands would move in; the Golden Tide would make them abundant; folk could live entirely off the chase, without falling back into savagery. Of course, the transition would take lifetimes, and those would be grim, but surely the star-beings would help. . . .

Thus it was daunting to see him shaken. "What do you mark, then?" Yewwl asked.

"I am not sure," Robreng confessed. "It's been too long since I was in snow-decked uplands. Once my partner went down in a deep drift and was stuck, but we got him out. Our guide took us well clear of high hillsides, but I can't recall why. He had few words of our language."

"Banner," Yewwl said aloud, each word a fog-puff, "do you know of any danger we might be in?"

Across hundreds of kilometers, the secret voice replied, "No. That doesn't mean there is none, you realize. Your world is so different from mine—and so few humans have visited it, really, in all these centuries—and now everything is changing so fast—How I wish I could warn you."

"Well, thank you, my oath-sister." Yewwl told Robreng what she had heard. Decision came. "I think I grasp what the matter is. It's within us—in me too. I remember how these parts were fair and alive when we were children; we remember caretakers, pilgrims, offerings and feasts and Oneness. Today we come back and find all gone dead and hollow. No wonder if dread arises." She straightened in her saddle. "Strike it down! Onward!"

Ych crossed a root of the mountain and dropped out of sight. In a moment, his shout rang over ice and rock. He had spied the Shrine.

His kin urged their onsars to speed, from shamble to swing. Four massive legs went to and fro; sparks flew where hoofs smote rock. Between, the thick extensors did more than help support the body; they gripped, pulled, shoved, let go, seized hold afresh on the ground. Aft of the hump where saddles or packs were, dorsal fins wagged, black triangles as high as a rider's head. Sweat gleamed on gray skin, sparse brown hair, big ears. Breath went loud, harsh, in and out of muzzles. Thews pulsed to the rocking motion.

Yewwl topped the ridge and glanced aloft. Sharply through the thin, clear air of the heights, she saw her goal.

The tomb of Kulembarach stood on a ledge a third of the way up the mountainside. It was a dolmen, rough granite slabs chiseled out of some quarry, somehow brought here and fitted together, in an age before iron. But around it, generation after generation had built terraces, raised houses and statues, nurtured exquisite gardens where fountains played and flutes replied. Here had been gathered the finest works of the clan and the best that traders abroad could bring home: pictures,

jewelry, weavings, books, such awesome memorabilia as the Sword Which Held the Bridge, Amarao's cup, the skulls of the Seven Heroes, the quern of Gro the Healer.

Today—

Nearing, Yewwl could barely make out the balustrades of the terraces, overflowed by snow. Frost had shattered several, and brought low a number of the sculptures which elsewhere stood forlorn as the stricken trees. When the last caretakers must depart or die, cold had numbed them into carelessness, fire had escaped a hearth, nothing but blackened stonework was left of the delicately carpentered buildings. Bereft of its wooden gate, the arch before the tomb gaped with horrible emptiness.

The onsars turned onto the road which led thither. It ascended too abruptly to be much drifted over, and the paving blocks were not yet sundered and tumbled and split, except in a few places. They rang under hoofs, answering the wind that wailed and bit and scattered a haze of dry ice crystals to shatter what sunlight came over the eastern shoulder into this darkling passage. Beyond the Shrine grounds the mountain rose steeper yet for a space, in a talus slope which clingplant had once made colorful but which was now only jagged and bleak. Above it, where the slope was easier, the snowpack began, that went on over the peak. It formed a white cliff, meters tall, mysteriously blue-shadowed.

Nonetheless . . . amidst the ruins, rearing over banks, upbearing what had fallen upon it during the night, the dolmen remained, foursquare. Kulembarach abided, at watch over her people. To those who sought her, she would still give dreams and luck . . . or, at least, the strength that came from remembering that she had prevailed in her day, and her blood endured. . . . Yewwl's pulse thuttered.

Ych was already there. When no keepers were left,

that had earned him the right to greet the Forebear on behalf of his party. He unslung the bugle at his saddlebow and put it to his lips. Riding around and around the tomb, he challenged desolation with the hunting call of his mother.

The snowcliff stirred.

A mighty wind rushed downward from it, smote like hammers, roared like thunder. Statues and tree boles toppled before the blow.

Earth shuddered. Hill-huge masses broke from the sliding precipice, flew, struck, smashed and buried what they hit. Behind them came the doom-fall itself.

Yewwl never remembered what happened. Surely she vaulted to a stance on her saddle and sprang from it, spreading her vanes, as if she were about to attack game on an open plain. Surely she went gliding, and she did not come down soon enough to be engulfed. Therefore surely she caught updrafts, rode the buffeting airs that the slide hurled before it, crashed bruised and bleeding but not truly wounded in her body, down onto a ridge above the path of destruction.

What she knew, at first, was nothing but a noise that should break the world apart, blindness, choked throat, tumbling well-nigh helpless—being tossed against raw rock and clawing herself fast while chaos raged—finally, silence, but for the ringing in her ears; and pain; and dazedly rising to stare.

Where the Shrine had been, the road, the onsars, her companions: snow filled the vale, nearly as high as she was. A mist of crystals swallowed vision within fifty meters; it would be hours in settling. Suddenly there was no wind, as if that also had been seized and overwhelmed.

"Robreng!" Yewwl screamed. "Ungn! Ych! Ngao!"

It took her hours of crawling about and shouting to become certain that none of them had escaped.

By then she was at the bottom of the slide, in the foothills under the mountain.

She staggered away. She would not rest before she must, before flesh and bones fell down in a heap. And then she would not be long a-swoon; she would rise again, again she would howl and snarl her sorrow, she would hunt and kill whatever stirred in the waste, because she could not kill the thing that had slain her darlings.

In Wainwright Station, Miriam Abrams slapped the switch of her multitransceiver, tore herself free of every connection to it, and surged from her chair. A calculator happened to be lying on the console shelf. She dashed it to the floor. It didn't break as she wanted, but it skittered. "God damn them!" she yelled. "God damn them to the deepest hole in hell!"

The single person in the room with her was Ivan Polevoy, electronician, who had had some tinkering to do on a different piece of equipment. He had seen Abrams rapt in her rapport with the native, but not what was happening, for side panels effectively blocked his view of the video screen. The woman maintained that her relationship was sufficient invasion of privacy—though she admitted "privacy" was a notion hard to apply between unlike species. She herself spent incredible lengths of time following the life of her subject. The Ramnuan obviously didn't mind, no matter how intimate events became. Possibly she'd not mind if other humans observed too. However, Abrams had made it plain from the start, a couple of decades ago, that she alone would receive the raw data. The reports she prepared on that basis were detailed, insightful contributions to xenology; but nobody else knew how much she chose to leave out.

The former chief of planetside operations had

supported her in that policy. It was doubtless prudent, when little was known about Ramnuan psychology. Nowadays Abrams was the chief, so the staff didn't object either. Besides, their own jobs or projects kept them amply busy, undermanned as the place was.

Hence Polevoy had to ask in surprise: "Damn who? What's wrong, Banner?"

It was as if her nickname calmed her a little. Yet she had borne it for many years. Translated from the local language—wherein it derived from the flag which identified Wainwright Station at a distance to travelers—it had practically supplanted "Miriam," even in her mind. At this hour, it seemed to tell her that dear ones died, but the race lived on.

Regardless, tears glistened on her lashes. The hand shook that fished a cigarette from a tunic pocket, struck it, and brought it to her mouth. Cheeks caved in with the violence of her smoking. Her voice was hoarse rather than husky, and wavered.

"Avalanche. Wiped out Yewwl's whole family . . . and, oh, God, the Shrine, the heart of her clan's history—like wiping out Jerusalem—" A fist beat itself unmercifully against the console. "I should have guessed. But . . . no experience. . . . I'm from Dayan, you know, warm, dry, no snow anywhere, and I've just been a visitor on worlds like Terra—" Her lips drew wide, her eyes squinched nearly shut. "If I'd thought! That much snowpack, and seven Terrestrial gravities to accelerate it—Yewwl, Yewwl, I'm sorry."

"Why, that's terrible," Polevoy said. After a pause: "Your subject, she's alive?"

Abrams jerked a nod. "Yes. With nothing to ride, no tent or supplies or tools or anything but what she's got on her person, and doubtless not a soul for a hundred kilometers around."

"Well, we'd better send a gravsled for her. It can home on her transceiver, can't it?" Polevoy was fairly new here.

"Sure, sure. Not right away, though. Don't you know what grief usually does to a Ramnuan? It's apt to drive him or her berserk." Abrams spoke in rough chunks of phrase. "Coping with that is a problem which every society on this planet has had to solve, one way or another. Maybe that's a main reason why they've never had wars—plenty of individual fights, but no wars, no armies, therefore no states—A soldier who lost his buddy would run amok." Laughter rattled from her. "Too bad we humans don't have the same trait. We wouldn't be cobwebbed into our Terran Empire then, would we?" She stubbed out the cigarette, viciously, and started the next. "We'll go fetch Yewwl when she's worked off the worst of what's in her, if she lives through it. Sometime this afternoon." That would be several standard days hence. "Meanwhile, I can be preparing to take on the wretched Empire."

Shocked, Polevoy could merely say, "I beg your pardon?"

Abrams slumped. She turned from him and stared out a viewscreen. It gave a broad overlook across the locality. On her right, the Kiiong River flowed seaward, more rapidly than any stream on Terra or Dayan would have gone through a bed as level as was here. Spray off rocks dashed brilliant above water made gray-green by glacial flour. Sonic receptors brought in a booming of great slow airs under more than thirty bars of pressure. Beyond the river was forest: low, thick trunks from which slender branches swayed, upheld by big leaves shaped like parachutes, surrounded by yellowish shrubs.

To her left, eastward, chanced to be rare clarity. Dun pyrasphale rippled across twelve kilometers to Ramnu's horizon. Trees and canebrakes broke the

sameness of that veldt; a kopje reared distance-blued; clouds cruised above, curiously flattened. A small herd of grazers wandered about, under guard of a mounted native. A score of flying creatures were aloft. When Abrams first arrived, this country had swarmed with life.

Overhead, the sky was milky. Niku, the sun, appearing two-thirds as wide as Sol seen from Terra, cast amber light; a frost halo circled it. Diris, the innermost moon, glimmered pale toward the west. It would not set until Ramnu's long day had become darkness.

"Another ice age on its way," Abrams mumbled. "The curse of this world. And we could stop it and all its kind. Whatever becomes of us and our Empire, we could be remembered as saviors, redeemers, for the next million years. But the Duke will not listen. And now Yewwl's people are dead."

"Uh," Polevoy ventured, "uh, doesn't she have a couple of children who're adult, married?"

"Yes. And *they* have children, who may well not survive what's coming down from the north," Abrams said. "Meanwhile she's lost her husband, her two youngsters, the last baby she'll ever bear; her clan has lost its Jerusalem; and none of that needed to happen." Tendons stood forth in her neck. "None of it! But the Grand Duke of Hermes would never listen to me!"

After more silence, she straightened, turned around, said quite calmly: "Well, I'm done with him. This has been the last thing necessary to decide me. I'm going to leave pretty soon, Ivan. Leave for Terra itself, and appeal for help to the very top."

Polevoy choked. "The Emperor?"

Abrams grinned in gallows mirth. "No, hardly him. Not at the start, anyhow. But . . . have you ever perchance heard of Admiral Flandry?"

II

First she must go to the Maian System, nineteen light-years off, a journey of four standard days in the poky little starcraft belonging to the Ramnu Research Foundation. The pilot bade her farewell at Williams Field on Hermes and went into Starfall to see what fleshpots he could find before returning. Banner also sought the planet's chief city, but with less frivolous intentions. Mainly she wanted shelter, and not from the mild climate.

She had cut her schedule as close as feasible. The liner *Queen of Apollo* would depart for Sol in fifty hours. Through Sten Runeberg, to whom she had sent a letter, she had a ticket. However, coming as she did from a primitive world of basically terrestroid biochemistry, she must get a checkup at a clinic licensed to renew her medical certificate. That was a ridiculous formality—even had she been exposed in shirtsleeves to Ramnu, no germ there could have lived a minute in her bloodstream—but the bureaucrats of Terra were adamant unless you held rank or title. Equally absurd, she thought, was the quasi-necessity of updating her wardrobe. She didn't think Flandry would care if she looked provincial. Yet others would, and her mission was difficult enough without her being at a psychological disadvantage.

Therefore she sallied forth on the morning after she arrived at the Runebergs' town house, and didn't come back, her tasks completed, till sundown. "You must be exhausted, fairling," said her host. "How about a drink before dinner?"

Fairling—The mild Hermetian endearment had taken on a special meaning for the two of them, when he was in charge of industrial operations at Ramnu and they had been lovers whenever they could steal time together. The three-year relationship had ended five years ago, with his inexplicable replacement by taciturn Nigel Broderick; it had never been deeply passionate; now he was married, and they had exchanged no more than smiles and glances during her stay, nor would they. Nonetheless, memory stabbed.

Runeberg's wife was belated at her office. He, who had become a consulting engineer, had quit work early for his guest and put his child in charge of the governess. He mixed two martinis himself and led the way onto a balcony. "Pick a seat," he invited, gesturing at a couple of loungers.

Banner stayed by the rail. "I'd forgotten how beautiful this is," she whispered.

Dusk flowed across the quicksilver gleam of Daybreak Bay. The mansion stood on the southern slope of Pilgrim Hill, near the Palomino River. It commanded a view of the keeps above; of its own garden, fragrant with daleflower and roses, where a tilirra flew trilling and glowflies were blinking alight; of Riverside Common, stately with million-leaf and rainroof trees; of multitudinous old spires beyond and windows that had begun to shine; of domes and towers across the stream, arrogantly radiant as if this were still that heyday of their world in which they had been raised. The air was barely cooled by a breeze and murmured only slightly of traffic. Heaven ranged from blue in the west to violet in the east. Antares was already visible, rising Venus-bright and ruby-red out of the Auroral Ocean.

"You should have come here more often," Runeberg said.

"You know I could hardly drag myself away from my work, ever, and then mostly to visit my parents," Banner replied. "Since Dad's death—" She broke off.

The big blond man regarded her carefully. She stood profile to, so that he saw the curve of her nose below the high forehead, the set of her wide mouth and the jut of her chin and the long sweep of her throat down to the small bosom. Clad in a shimmerlyn gown—for practice at being a lady, she had said—she stood tall and slim, athletic despite the scattered silver in a shoulder-length light-brown mane. Then she turned around, briefly silhouetting a cheekbone ivory against the sky, and her eyes confronted his. They were perhaps her best feature, large and luminous green under dark brows.

"Yes," he blurted, "you've let yourself get crazily wrapped up in those beings. Sometimes I'd find you slipping into styles of thought, emotion, that, well, that weren't human. It must have gotten worse since I left. Come back, Miri."

He disliked calling me Banner, she remembered. "You imply that involvement with an intelligent, feeling race was bad in the first place," she said. "Why? On the whole, I've had a wonderful, fascinating, exciting life. And how else can we get to understand them? A different psychology, explored in depth. . . . What can we not learn, also about ourselves?"

Runeberg sighed. "Who is really paying attention? Be honest. You're studying one clutch of sophonts among countless thousands; and they're barbarians, impoverished, insignificant. Their planet was always more interesting to science than they were, and it was investigated centuries back, in plenty of detail. Xenology is a dying discipline anyway. Every pure science is; we live in that kind of era. Why do you think your foundation is marginally funded? Hai-ah, it'd have been closed down before you were born, if Ramnu didn't happen to have some value to Hermetian industry. You've sacrificed every heritage that was yours—for what, Miri?"

"We've wasted time on that battleground in the past," she snapped. Her tone softened. "I don't want to quarrel, Sten. You mean well, I know. From your viewpoint, I suppose you're right."

"I care about you, my very dear friend," he said.

And it hurt you from the start to learn what I'd lost, she did not answer aloud. *My marriage*—Already established in the profession when he took a fresh graduate from the Galactic Academy for his bride, Feodor Sumarokov had seen their appointments to Ramnu as a steppingstone to higher positions; when he left after three years, she would not. *My true love*—She had never wedded Jason Kamunya, because they wanted to do that back on Dayan where her parents were, and somehow they never found a time when so long an absence wouldn't harmfully interrupt their research, and meanwhile they could live and work together . . . until that day in their fourth year when a stone falling from a height under seven gravities shattered his air helmet and head. . . . *My chance for children*—Well, perhaps not yet. She was only forty-four. But not all the gero treatment known to man could stave off menopause for more than a decade, or add more than two or three to a lifespan; and where she was, she had had access to nothing but routine cell therapy. *My home, my kindred, my whole civilization*—

Ramnu is my home! Yewwl and her folk are my kin in everything but flesh. And what is Technic civilization worth any longer? Unless I can make it save my oath-sister's world.

Banner smiled and reached out to stroke the man's cheek. "Thank you for that," she murmured.

"And for a lot else." Raising her glass: *"Shalom."*

Rims clinked together. The liquor was cold and pungent on her tongue. She and he reclined facing each other. Twilight deepened.

"You completed your business today?" he inquired.

"Yes. Inconspicuously, I hope."

He frowned. "You really are obsessive about secrecy, aren't you?"

"Or forethoughtful." Her voice wavered the least bit. "Sten, you did do your best to handle my reservation and such confidentially, didn't you?"

"Of course, since you asked. I'm not sure why you did."

"I explained. If the Duke knew, he might well decide to stop me. And he could, in a dozen different ways."

"Why would he, though?"

Banner took a protracted sip. Her free hand fumbled in her sash pocket for a cigarette case. "He's neutronium-solid set against any project to reverse the glaciation on Ramnu."

"Hoy? . . . True, true, you complained to me, in person and afterward in those rare letters you sent, that he won't consider Hermes making the effort." Runeberg drew breath for an argument. "Maybe he is being ungenerous. We could afford it. But he may well deem—in fact, you've quoted him to me to that effect—that our duty to ourselves is overriding. Hermes isn't poor, but it's not the rich, powerful world it used to be, either, and we're developing plenty of problems, both domestic and *vis-à-vis* the Imperium. I can understand how Duke Edwin may think an expensive undertaking for the sake of aliens who can never pay us back—how that might strain us dangerously, rouse protest, maybe even provoke an attempt at revolution."

Banner started her smoke before she said bitterly,

"Yes, he must feel insecure, yes, indeed. It's not as if he belonged to the House of Tamarin, or as if constitutional government still existed here. His grandfather was the latest in a string of caudillos, and he himself eased his elder brother off the throne."

"Now, wait," Runeberg protested. "You realize I'm not too happy with him either. But he is doing heroic things for Hermes, and he does have ample popular support. If he has no Tamarin genes in him, he does carry a few Argolid ones, distantly, but from the Founder of the Empire just the same. It's the Imperium that's jeopardized its own right to rule—Hans Molitor seizing the crown by force—later robbing us of Mirkheim, to buy the goodwill of the money lords on Terra—" He checked himself. It was talk heard often nowadays, in private. But he didn't want to speak anger this evening. Moreover, she was leaving tomorrow in hopes of getting help there.

"The point is," he said, "why should the Duke mind having your project financed and organized from outside? He ought to welcome that. Most of the resources and labor could come from our economic sphere. We'd get nice jobs, profits, contacts, every sort of benefit."

"I don't know why he should object," Banner admitted. "I do know he will, if he finds out. I've exchanged enough letters and tapes with his immediate staff. I've come in person, twice, to plead, and got private audiences both times. Oh, the responses were more or less courteous, but always absolutely negative; and meeting with him, I could sense outright hostility."

Runeberg gulped from his drink before he ventured to say: "Are you sure you weren't reading that into his manner? No offense, fairling, but you are not too well acquainted with humankind."

"I've objective facts in addition, in full measure,"

she retorted. "My last request was that he ask the Emperor to aid Ramnu. His answer, through an undersecretary, was that this would be politically inadvisable. I'm not too naive to recognize when I'm being fobbed off. Especially when the message closed by stating that they were tired of this business, and if I persisted in it I could be replaced. Edwin Cairncross is quite willing to use his influence on Terra to crush one obscure scientist!"

She drew hard on her cigarette, leaned forward, and continued: "That's not the only clue. For instance, why were you discharged from General Enterprises? Everybody I talked to was astounded. You'd been doing outstanding work."

"I was simply told 'reorganization,'" he reminded her. "I did get handsome severance pay and testimonials. As near as I've been able to find out, somebody in a high position wanted Nigel Broderick to have my post. Bribery? Blackmail? Nepotism? Who knows?"

"Broderick's been less and less cooperative with the Foundation," she said. "And that in spite of his expanding operations on Ramnu as well as its moons. Though it's impossible to learn exactly what the expansion amounts to. The time is past when my people or I could freely visit any of those installations."

"Um-m, security precautions—There's been a lot of restriction in the Protectorate, too, lately. These are uneasy years. If the Imperium breaks down again—which could give the Merseians a chance to strike—"

"What threat to security is a xenological research establishment? But we're being denied adequate supplies, that we used to get as a matter of course from Dukeston and Elaveli. The pretexts are mighty thin, stuff like unspecified 'technical difficulties.' Sten, we're being slowly strangled. The Duke wants us severely restricted in our activities on both Ramnu and Diris, if not out of there altogether. Why?"

Banner finished her cigarette and reopened the case. "You smoke too much, Miri," Runeberg said.

"And drink too little?" Her laugh clanked. "Very well, let's assume my troubles have made me paranoid. What harm in keeping alert? If I return in force, maybe my questions will get answered."

He raised his brows. "In force?"

"Oh, not literally. But with backing too powerful for a mere lord of a few planetary systems."

"Whose backing?"

"Haven't you heard me mention Admiral Flandry?"

"Ye-es, occasionally in conversation, I believe. I got the impression he is—was a friend of your father's."

"Dad was his first superior in action, during the Starkad affair," she said proudly. "He got him started in Naval Intelligence. They kept in touch afterward. I met Flandry myself, as a girl, when he paid a visit to a base where Dad was stationed. I liked him, and he wouldn't have stayed Dad's friend if he weren't a decent man at heart, no matter what he may have had to do in his career. He'll receive a daughter of Max Abrams. And . . . he has the Emperor's ear."

She tossed down her cigarette case, raised her glass, and said almost cheerfully, "Come, let's drink to my success, and then let's hear more about what's been happening to you, Sten, old dear."

Night rolled westward across Greatland. Four hours after it had covered Starfall it reached Lythe, in the middle of the continent.

That estate of Edwin Cairncross, Grand Duke of Hermes, was among his most cherished achievements. Reclamation of the interior for human settlement had faltered a century ago, as the wealth and importance of the planet declined. Civil war had stopped it entirely, and it had not resumed at once after Hans Molitor battered the Empire back together. He, Cairncross, had seen an extinct shield volcano rising mightily above an arid steppe, and desired an eyrie on the heights. He had decreed that canals be driven, land be resculptured and planted, lovely ornithoids and big game be introduced, a town be founded down below and commerce make it prosper. The undertaking was minor compared to other works of his, but somehow, to him, Lythe symbolized the will to prevail, to conquer.

It was no sanctuary for fantasy, but a nucleus for renewed growth. From it he did considerable of his governing, through an electronic web that reached across the globe and beyond. An invitation to spend some days here could be portentous. This evening he had passed hours alone in his innermost office, hunched above the screen whose sealed circuits brought him information gathered by a bare dozen secret agents. They were the elite of their corps; they reported directly to him, and he decided if their nominal superiors would be told.

Now he must make a heavier choice than that. With a blind urge to draw strength from his land, he strode out of the room and through the antechambers.

Beyond, a sentry snapped a salute. Cairncross returned it as precisely. His years in the Imperial Navy had taught him that a leader is wise to give his underlings every courtesy due them. An aide sprang from a chair and inquired, "Sir?"

"I don't want to be disturbed, Wyatt," Cairncross said.

"Sir!"

Cairncross nodded and went on down the hall.

Until new orders came, the lieutenant would make sure that nobody, not the Duchess herself, got near the Grand Duke.

A gravshaft brought Cairncross up onto a tower. He crossed its deck and halted at the battlement. That was pure ornamentation, but not useless; he had ordered it built because he wanted to feel affirmed in his kinship to Shi Huang Ti, Charlemagne, Suleiman the Magnificent, Pyotr the Great, every man who had ever been dominant on Terra.

Silence dwelt enormous. The fog of his breath caught the light of a crescent Sandalion; he savored the bracing chill that he inhaled. Vision winged across roofs, walls, hoar treetops, cliffs and crags, a misty shimmer of plains, finally the horizon. He raised his eyes and beheld stars in their thousands.

Antares burned brightest. Mogul was sufficiently near to rival it, an orange spark: Mogul, sun of Babur, the Protectorate. His gaze did not seek Olga, for in that constellation, invisible to him, was the black sun of Mirkheim; and he had no time on hand to think about regaining the treasure planet for Hermes. Sol was hidden too, by distance. But Sol— Terra—was ruler of the rest. . . . He turned his glance from the Milky Way. Its iciness declared that the Empire was an incident upon certain attendants of a hundred thousand stars, lost in the outskirts of a galaxy which held more than a hundred billion. A man must ignore mockery.

Wryness: *A man must also buckle down to practical details.* What Cairncross had learned today demanded instant action.

The trouble was, he could not do the quick and simple thing. Abrams had been too wary. His fists knotted.

Thank God for giving him the foresight to have Sten Runeberg's house bugged, after he'd gotten the man fired from Ramnu. Not that Runeberg had made

trouble. He might have, though. The family was extensive and influential; Duchess Iva was a second cousin of Sten. And he had been at Ramnu, he had been close to Abrams, he had surely acquired ideas from her . . . and maybe worse ones afterward, since they did irregularly correspond and meet.

Nothing worth reporting had happened until today. But what finally came was a blow to the guts.

The witch outmaneuvered me, Cairncross thought. *I have the self-confidence to realize that.* She'd written to Runeberg in care of the spaceship he used in his business; no bug could escape the safety inspections there. She'd arrived unannounced and gone straight to his place. The ducal government lacked facilities to monitor every slightly distrusted site continuously; tapes were scanned at intervals. Given reasonable luck, Abrams would have been in and out of Hermes well before Cairncross knew.

She did chance to pick the wrong time slot. (That was partly because surveillance was programmed to intensify whenever a passenger liner was due in, until it had departed.) But she had anticipated the possibility. Runeberg and a couple of his spacemen were going to escort her tomorrow, not just onto the shuttle but to the *Queen* in orbit, and see her off. He had objected that that was needless, but to soothe her he had agreed. Meanwhile, his wife and several others knew about it all. There was no way, under these conditions, to arrange an abduction or assassination. Anything untoward would be too damnably suspicious, in a period when a degree of suspicion was already aimed at Cairncross.

Well, I've made my own contingency plans. I didn't foresee this turn of events exactly, but—

Decision crystallized. *Yes, I'll go to Terra myself. My speedster can outrun her by days.*

Cairncross made a fighting grin. Whatever came next should at least be interesting!

III

Vice Admiral Sir Dominic Flandry, Intelligence Corps, Imperial Terran Navy, maintained three retreats in different areas that he liked. None was as sybaritic as his home base in Archopolis, a part of which served him for an office. A part of that, in turn, was austere, for times when he found it helpful to give such an impression of himself. Which room he used seldom mattered; ordinarily he did his business through computers, infotrieves, and eidophone, with the latter set to show no background. Some people, though, must be received in person. A governing noble who wanted to see him privately was an obvious example.

This meant rising at an unsanctified hour—after a visitor had kept him awake past midnight—to review available data in advance of the appointment. The visitor had been warned she must go before breakfast, since he couldn't afford the time for gallantries. Flandry left her drowsy warmth and a contrail of muttered curses behind him, groped his way to the gymnasium, and plunged. A dozen laps around the pool brought him to alertness. They failed to make the exercises which followed any fun. He had loathed calisthenics more in every successive year of his sixty-one. But they had given him a quickly responsive body in his youth, and it was still trim and tough beyond anything due to gero treatments.

At last he could shower. When he emerged, Chives proffered a Turkish towel and coffee royal. "Good morning, sir," he greeted.

Flandry took the cup. "That phrase is a contradiction in terms," he said. "How are you doing?"

"Quite well, thank you, sir." Chives began to rub his master dry. He wasn't as deft as erstwhile. He didn't notice that he nearly caused the coffee to spill. Flandry kept silence. Had he, in this place, let anyone but Chives attend him, the Shalmuan's heart would have cracked open.

Flandry regarded the short green form—something like a hairless human with a long tail, if you ignored countless differences in shapes and proportions of features—through eyes that veiled concern. This early, Chives wore merely a kilt. Wrinkles, skinniness, stiff movements were far too plain to sight. No research institution had ever considered developing the means to slow down aging in the folk of his backward world.

Well, if that were done, how many other sophont races would clamor for the same work on each of their wildly separate biochemistries? the man thought, for perhaps the thousandth sad time. *I may have my valet-majordomo-cook-bodyguard-pilot-factotum-arbiter for a decade yet, if I'm lucky.*

Chives finished and gave the towel a reassuringly vigorous snap. "I have laid out your formal uniform and decorations, sir," he announced.

"Formal—one cut below court? And decorations? He'll take me for a popinjay."

"My impression of the Duke is otherwise, sir."

"When did you get at his dossier? . . . Never mind. No use arguing."

"I suggest you be ready for breakfast in twenty minutes, sir. There will be a soufflé."

"Twenty minutes on the dot. Very good, Chives." Flandry left.

As usual when it was unoccupied, the clothes were in a guestroom. Flandry draped them over his tall frame with the skill of a foppish lifetime. These days, he didn't really care—had not since a lady died on Dennitza, fourteen years ago—but remained a fashion plate out of habit, and because it was expected of him. Deep-blue tunic, gold on collar and sleeves, nebula and star on either shoulder; scarlet sash; white iridon trousers bagged into half-boots of lustrous black beefleather; and the assorted ribbons, of course, each a brag about an exploit though most of the citations were recorded only in the secret files; and the Imperial sunburst, jewel-encrusted, hung from his neck, to proclaim him a member of the Order of Manuel, silliest boast of the lot—

Brushing his sleek iron-gray hair, he checked to make sure his last dash of beard inhibitor wasn't wearing off. It wasn't, but he decided to trim the mustache that had, thus far, stayed brown. The face behind hadn't changed much either: high in the cheekbones, straight in the nose, cleft in the chin, relic of a period when everybody who could afford it got biosculped into comeliness. (The present generation scorned that; in many ways, these were puritanical times.) The eyes of changeable gray were more clear than they deserved to be after last night. The skin, lightly tanned, stayed firm, though lines ran over the brow, crow's-feet beneath, deep furrows from nostrils to lips.

Yes, he thought a trifle smugly, *we're holding our own against the Old Man.* A sudden, unexpected thrust brought a gasp. *Why not? What's his hurry? He's hauled in Kossara and young Dominic and Hans and—how many more? I can be left to wait his convenience.*

He rallied. *Self-pity! First sign of senility? Squash it, fellow. You've got health, money, power, friends, women, interesting work that you can even claim is of some importance if you want to. Your breakfast is being prepared by none less than Chives —* He glanced at his watch, whistled, and made haste to the dining room.

The Shalmuan met him at the entrance. "Excuse me, sir," he said, and reached up to adjust the sunburst on its ribbon before he seated his master and went to bring the food.

The weather bureau had decreed a fine spring day. Chives had therefore retracted the outer wall. Flowers, Terran and exotic, made the roof garden beyond into an explosion of colors and perfumes. A Cynthian yaoti perched bright-plumed on a bough of a blossoming orange tree and harped out of its throat. Everywhere around, towers soared heavenward in fluid grace; this quarter of the city went back two centuries, to when an inspired school of architecture had flourished. White clouds wandered through blue clarity; aircars sparkled in sunlight. A breeze brought coolness and a muted pulse of machines in the service of man. And here came the soufflé.

Later was the first, the truly delicious cigarette, out in the garden beside a dancing fountain. What followed was less pleasant, namely, spadework. But all this had to be paid for somehow. Flandry could retire whenever he chose: to a modest income from pension and investments, and an early death from boredom. He preferred to stay in the second oldest profession. In between adventures and enjoyments, an Intelligence officer—a spy—must needs do a vast amount of grubby foundation-laying.

He sought the fancier office and keyed for information on Edwin Cairncross, Grand Duke of Hermes. That meant a historical and social review of the planet itself.

The sun, Maia (not to be confused with giant 20 Tauri), was in Sector Antares. Its attendants included a terrestroid globe which had been colonized early on, largely by northern Europeans. Basic conditions, including biology, were homelike enough that the settlement did well. The inevitable drawbacks included the concentration of most land in a single huge continent whose interior needed modification—for instance, entire systems of rivers and lakes to relieve its aridity—before it was fit for humans to live in. Meanwhile they prospered along the coasts. Originally their polity was a rather curious development out of private corporations, with a head of state elected from a particular family to serve for life or good behavior. Society got stratified in the course of time, and reaction against that was fuelled by the crisis that the Babur War brought. Reforms turned Hermes into an ordinary type of crowned republic.

The war had also resulted in making it an interstellar power. It assumed protectorship over the defeated Baburites; they were too alien for close relations, but what there were, political and commercial, appeared to have been pretty amicable through the centuries. Hermetians started colonies and enterprises in several nearby systems. Most significantly, they had stewardship of Mirkheim, the sole known source of supermetals.

They needed their wealth and strength, for the Troubles were upon Technic civilization. Wars, revolutions, plundering raids raged throughout its space. Hermes must often fight. This led to a military-oriented state and a concentration of authority in the executive. When at last Manuel had established the Terran Empire and its Pax was spreading afar, that state was able to join on highly favorable terms.

Afterward . . . well, naturally the files couldn't

say so, but as the Empire decayed, Hermes did too. Again and again, lordship went to the man with the armed force to take it. The economy declined, the sphere of influence shrank. Hans Molitor finally reasserted the supremacy of Terra. Generally he was welcomed by folk weary of chaos. But he had political debts to pay, and one payment involved putting lucrative Mirkheim directly under the Imperium. It was then a reasonable precaution to reduce sharply the autonomy of the Grand Duchy, disband its fighting services, require its businesses to mesh with some elsewhere—which worsened resentment. Riots erupted and Imperial agents were murdered, before the Marines restored order.

Today's Duke, Edwin Cairncross, appeared properly submissive; but appearances were not very reliable across a couple of hundred light-years, and certainly he had several odd items in his record. Now fifty-five, he had been the youngest son by a second marriage of a predecessor who gave Hans much trouble before yielding. Thus he had no obvious prospect of becoming more than a member of the gentry. Reviving an old Hermetian tradition, he enlisted in the Imperial Navy for a five-year hitch and left it bearing the rank of lieutenant commander. That was only partly due to family; he had served well, earning promotions during the suppression of the Nyanzan revolt and in the Syrax confrontation.

Returning home, he embarked energetically on a number of projects. Among these, he enlarged what had been a petty industrial operation on the strange planet Ramnu and its moons. Meanwhile he held a succession of political posts and built up support for himself. Ten years ago, he became ready to compel the abdication of his older half-brother and his own election to the throne. Since then, he had put various measures into effect and undertaken various public works that were popular.

Hence on the surface, he seemed a desirable man in his position. The staff of the Imperial legate on Hermes were less sure of that. Their reports over the past decade showed increasing worry. Cairncross' image, writings, recorded speeches were everywhere. Half the adolescents on the home globe joined an organization which was devoted to outdoorsmanship and sports but which was called the Cairncross Pioneers; its counselors preached a patriotism that was integral with adoration of him. Scholars were prodded into putting on symposia about his achievements and his prospects for restoring the greatness of his people. News media trumpeted his glories.

None of this was actually subversive. Many local lords exhibited egomania but were otherwise harmless. However, it was a possible danger signal. The impression was reinforced by the legate's getting no more exact information than law required—on space traffic, demography, production and distribution of specified goods, etc.—and his agents being unable to gather more for themselves or even ascertain whether what they were given was accurate. "We respect the right of individual choice here" was the usual bland response to an inquiry. The Babur Protectorate had been virtually sealed off: ostensibly at the desire of the natives, who were not Imperial subjects and therefore were free to demand it; but how could an outsider tell? Anything might be in preparation, anywhere throughout a volume of space that included scores of suns. Recent messages from the legate urged that Terra mount a full investigation.

The recommendation has drowned, Flandry thought, *in the data, pleas, alarms that come here from a hundred thousand worlds. It has never gotten anywhere near the attention of the Policy Board. No lower-echelon official has flagged it. Why should he? Hermes is far off, close to that march of the Empire. By no possibility could it muster the power to make itself independent again, let alone pose any serious threat to Terra. The clearly dangerous cases are too many, too many.*

Is there a danger, anyway . . . when the Duke has arrived of his free will and wants to see me, of all unlikely candidates?

Flandry searched for personal items. They were surprisingly few, considering what a cult the chap had built around himself. Cairncross was long married, but childlessly; indications were that that was due to a flaw in him, not his wife. Yet he had never cloned, which seemed odd for an egotist unless you supposed that his vainglory was too much for him to make such an admission. He was a mighty womanizer, but usually picked his bedmates from the lower classes and took care to keep them humble. Men found him genial when he was in the right mood, though always somewhat overawing, and terrifying when he grew angry. He had no close friends, but was generally considered to be trustworthy and a just master. He was an ardent sportsman, hunter, crack shot; he piloted his own spacecraft and had explored lethally unterrestroid environments; he was an excellent amateur cabinetmaker; his tastes were fairly simple, except that he enjoyed and understood wine; distilled beverages he consumed a bit heavily, without showing any effects; he was not known to use more drugs than alcohol—

Flandry decided to receive him in this office.

"Welcome, your Grace."

"Thank you." A firm handshake ended. Cairncross was putting on no airs.

"Please be seated. May I offer your Grace refreshments? I'm well stocked."

"M-m-m . . . Scotch and soda, then. And let's drop the titles while we're the two of us. I aim to talk frankly."

Chives shimmered in and took orders. Cairncross stared curiously after the Shalmuan—probably he'd never met any before—and swung attention back to his host. "Well, well," he said. "So this is the legendary Admiral Flandry."

"No, the objectively real Admiral Flandry, I hope. Some would say objectionably real."

Cairncross formed a smile and a chuckle, both short-lived. "The objectors have ample cause," he said. "Thank God for that."

"Indeed?"

"They've been our enemies, haven't they? I know why you got that medallion you're wearing. The business wasn't publicized—would've been awkward for diplomacy, right?—but a man in my kind of position has ways of learning things if he's interested. You pulled the fangs of the Merseians at Chereion, and we no longer have to worry about them."

Flandry quelled a wince, for that episode had cost him heavily. "Oh, but I'm afraid we do," he said. "Their Intelligence apparatus suffered severe damage, true. However, nothing else did, and they're hard at work rebuilding it. They'll be giving us fun and games again."

"Not if we stay strong." Cairncross' gaze probed and probed. "Which is basically what I'm here about."

Flandry returned the look. Cairncross was tall and broad, with a tigerish suppleness to his movements. His face was wide on a wedge-shaped cranium, Roman-nosed, thin-lipped, fully debearded. The hair was red and starting to get scant, the eyes pale blue, the complexion fair and slightly freckled. His voice was deep and sonorous, crisply accented. He was wearing ordinary civilian garb, blouse and trousers in subdued hues, but a massive ring of gold and emerald sparkled on a furry finger.

Flandry lighted a cigarette. "Pray proceed," he invited.

"Strength demands unity," Cairncross replied. "Out my way, unity is threatened. I believe you can save it."

Chives brought the whisky, a glass of white Burgundy, and canapés. When he had gone, the Duke resumed in a rush:

"You'll have checked my dossier. You're aware that I'm somewhat under suspicion. I've listened to your legate often enough; he makes no direct accusations, but he complains. Word that he sends here gets back to me through channels you can easily guess at. And I doubt if I'll shock you by saying that, in self-defense, I've sicced agents of mine onto agents of the Imperium on Hermes, to learn what they're doing and conjecturing. Am I secretly preparing for a revolt, a coup, or what? They wonder, yes, they wonder very hard."

"Being suspected of dreadful things is an occupational hazard of high office, isn't it?" Flandry murmured.

"But I'm innocent!" Cairncross protested. "I'm loyal! The fact of my presence on Terra—"

His tone eased: "I've grown more and more troubled about this. Finally I've decided to take steps. I'm taking them myself, rather than sending a representative, because, frankly, I'm not sure who I can trust any more.

"You know how impossible it is for a single man, no matter what power he supposedly has, to control everything, or know most of what's going on. Underlings can evade, falsify, conceal, drag their feet; your most useful officials can be conspirators against you, biding their time—Well, you understand, Admiral.

"I've begun to think there actually is a conspiracy on Hermes. In that case, I am its sacrifical goat."

Flandry trickled smoke ticklingly through his nostrils. "What do you mean, please?" he asked, though he thought he knew.

He was right. "Take an example," Cairncross said. "The legate wants figures on our production of palladium and where it is consumed. My government isn't technically required to provide that information, but it is required to cooperate with the representative of the Imperium, and his request for those figures is reasonable under the circumstances. After all, palladium is essential to protonic control systems, which are essential to any military machine. Now can I, personally, supply the data? Of course not. But when his agents try to collect them, and fail, I get blamed."

"No offense," Flandry said, "but you realize that, theoretically, the guilt could trace back to you. If you'd issued the right orders to the right individuals—"

Cairncross nodded. "Yes. Yes. That's the pure hell of it.

"I don't know if the plotters mean to discredit me so that somebody else can take my title, or if something worse is intended. I can't prove there *is* a plot. Maybe not; maybe it's an unfortunate set of coincidences. But I do know my good name is being gnawed away. I also know this kind of thing—disunity—can only harm the Empire. I've come for help."

Flandry savored his wine. "I sympathize," he said. "What can I do?"

"You're known to the Emperor."

Flandry sighed. "That impression dies hard, doesn't it? I was moderately close to Hans. After he

died, Dietrich consulted me now and then, but not
frequently. And I'm afraid Gerhart doesn't like me a
whole lot."

"Well, still, you have influence, authority, reputation."

"These days, I have what amounts to a roving
commission, and I can call on resources of the
Corps. That's all."

"That's plenty!" Cairncross exclaimed. "See here.
What I want is an investigation that will exonerate
me and turn up whatever traitors are nested in

Hermes. It would look peculiar if I suddenly appeared before the Policy Board and demanded this; it would damage me politically at home, as you can well imagine. But a discreet investigation, conducted by a person of unimpeachable loyalty and ability—Do you see?"

Loyalty? passed through Flandry. *To what? Scarcely to faithless Gerhart; scarcely even to this walking corpse of an Empire. Well, to the Pax, I suppose; to some generations of relative security that people can use to live in, before the Long Night falls; to my corps and my job, which have given me quite a bit of satisfaction; to a certain tomb on Dennitza, and to various memories.*

"I can't issue several planets a clean bill of health just by myself," he said.

"Oh, no," Cairncross answered. "Gather what staff you need. Take as much time as you like. You'll get every kind of cooperation I'm able to give. If you don't get it from elsewhere, well, isn't that what your mission will be about?"

"Hm." *I have been idle for a while. It is beginning to pall. Besides, I've never been on Hermes; and from what little I know about them, planets like Babur and Ramnu may prove fascinating.* "It definitely interests; and, as you say, it could affect a few billion beings more than you. What have you in mind, exactly?"

"I want you and your immediate aides to come back with me at once," Cairncross said. "I've brought my yacht; she's fast. I realize that'll be too few personnel, but you can reconnoiter and decide what else to send for."

"Isn't this rather sudden?"

"Damn it," Cairncross exploded, "I've been strangling in the net for years! We may not have much time left." Calmer: "Your presence would help by itself. We'd not make a spectacle of it, of

course, but the right parties—starting with his Majesty's legate—would know you'd come, and feel reassured."

"A moment, please, milord." Flandry stretched out an arm and keyed his infotrieve. What he wanted flashed onto the screen.

"The idea tempts," he said, "assuming that one can be tempted to do a good deed. You'll understand that I'd have arrangements to make first. Also, I've grown a smidgin old for traveling on a doubtless comfortless speedster; and I might want assistants from the start who themselves cannot leave on short notice." He waved a hand. "This is assuming I undertake the assignment. I'll have to think further about that. But as for a preliminary look-see, well, I note that the *Queen of Apollo* arrives next week. She starts back to Hermes three days later, and first class accommodations are not filled. We can talk *en route*. Your crew can take your boat home."

Cairncross flushed. He smote the arm of his seat. "Admiral, this is an Imperial matter. It cannot wait."

"It has waited, by your account," Flandry drawled. Instinct, whetted throughout a long career, made him add: "Besides, I need answers to a hundred questions before I can know whether I ought to do this."

"You will do it!" Cairncross declared. Catching his breath: "If need be—the Emperor is having a reception for me, the normal thing. I'll speak to him about this if you force me to. I would prefer, for your sake, that you don't get a direct order from the throne; but I can arrange it if I must."

"Sir," Flandry purred, while his inwardness uncoiled itself for action, "my apologies. I meant no disrespect. You've simply taken me by surprise. Please think. I've commitments of my own. In fact, considering them, I realize they require my absence for about two weeks. After that, I can probably make for Hermes in my personal craft. When I've conducted enough interviews and studies there, I should know who else to bring."

He lifted his glass. "Shall we discuss details, milord?"

Hours later, when Cairncross had left, Flandry thought: *Oh, yes, something weird is afoot in Sector Antares.*

Perhaps the most suggestive thing was his reaction to my mention of the Queen of Apollo. *He tried to hide it, but. . . . Now who or what might be aboard her?*

IV

Banner had not seen Terra since she graduated at the age of twenty-one, to marry Sumarokov and depart for Ramnu. Moreover, the Academy had been an intense, largely self-contained little world, from which cadets seldom found chances to venture during their four years. She had not hankered to, either. Childhood on Dayan, among the red-gold Tammuz Mountains, followed by girlhood as a Navy brat in the strange outposts where her father got stationed, had not prepared her for any gigapolis. Nor had her infrequent later visits to provincial communities. Starfall, the biggest, now seemed like a village, nearly as intimate and unterrifying as Bethyaakov her birthplace.

She had made acquaintances in the ship. A man among them had told her a number of helpful facts, such as the names of hotels she could afford in the capital. He offered to escort her around as well, but his kindnesses were too obviously in aid of getting her into bed, and she resented that. Only one of her few affairs had been a matter of real love, but none had been casual.

Thus she found herself more alone, more daunted among a million people and a thousand towers, than ever in a wildwood or the barrenness of a moon. Maybe those numbers, million, thousand, were wrong. It felt as if she could see that many from the groundside terminal, but she was dazed. She did know that they went on beyond sight, multi-plied over and over around the curve of the planet. Archopolis was merely a nexus; no matter if the globe had blue oceans and green open spaces— some huge, being property of nobility—it was a single city.

She collected her modest baggage, hailed a cab, blurted her destination to the autopilot, and fled. In nightmare beauty, the city gleamed, surged, droned around her.

At first the Fatima Caravanserai seemed a refuge. It occupied the upper third of an unpretentious old building, and had itself gone dowdy; yet it was quiet, reasonably clean, adequately equipped, and the registry desk held a live clerk, not a machine, who gave her cordial greeting and warned against the fish in the restaurant; the meat was good, he said.

But when she entered her room and the door slid shut, suddenly it was as though the walls drew close.

Nonsense! she told herself. *I'm tired and tense. I need to relax, and this evening have a proper dinner, with wine and the works.*

And who for company?

That question chilled. Solitude had never before oppressed her. If anything, she tended to be too independent of her fellow humans. But it was horri-ble to find herself an absolute stranger in an entire world.

Nonsense! she repeated. *I do know Admiral Flan-dry . . . slightly. . . . Will he remember me? No doubt several of my old instructors are still around. . . . Are they? The Xenological Society maintains a clubhouse, and my name may strike a chord in somebody if I drop in. . . . Can it?*

A cigarette between her lips, she began a whirl of unpacking. Thereafter a hot shower and a soft robe gave comfort. She blanked the viewer wall and keyed for a succession of natural scenes and historic monuments which the infotrieve told her was available, plus an excellent rendition of the pipa music she particularly enjoyed. The conveyor delivered a stiff cognac as ordered. Local time was 1830; in a couple of hours she might feel like eating. Now she settled down in a lounger to ease off.

No. She remained too restless. Rising, prowling, she reached the phone. There she halted. For a moment her fingers wrestled each other. It would likely be pointless to try calling Flandry before tomorrow. And then she could perhaps spend days getting her message through. A prominent man on Terra must have to live behind a shield-burg of subordinates.

Well, what harm in finding out the number?

That kept the system busy for minutes, since she did not know how to program its search through the bureaucratic structure. No private listing turned up, nor had she expected any. Two strings of digits finally flashed onto the screen. The first was coded for "Office," the second for "Special."

Was the latter an answering service? In that case, she could record her appeal immediately.

To her surprise, a live face appeared, above a uniform that sported twin silver comets on the shoulders. To her amazement, though the Anglic she heard was unmistakably Terran, the person was an alert-looking young woman. Banner had had the idea that Terran women these days were mostly ornaments, drudges, or whores. "Lieutenant Okuma," she heard. "May I help you?"

"I—well, I—" Banner collected herself. "Yes, please. I'm anxious to get in touch with Admiral Flandry. It's important. If you'll tell him my name, Miriam Abrams, and remind him I'm the daughter of Max Abrams, I'm sure he—"

"Hold on!" Okuma rapped. "Have you newly arrived?''

"Yes, a few hours ago.''

"On the *Queen of Apollo?*''

"Why, yes, but—''

"Have you contacted anybody else?''

"Only customs and immigration officers, and the hotel staff, and—'' Banner bridled. "What does this mean?''

"Excuse me,'' Okuma said. "I believe it means a great deal. I've been manning this line all day. Don't ask me why; I've not been told.'' She leaned forward. Her manner intensified. "Would you tell me where you are and what you want?''

"Fatima Caravanserai, Room 776,'' Banner blurted, "and I'm hoping he'll use his influence on behalf of a sophont species that desperately needs help. The Grand Duke of Hermes has refused it, so—'' Her words faltered, her heart stammered.

"Grand Duke, eh? . . . Enough,'' Okuma said. "Please pay attention. Admiral Flandry has been called away on business. Where, has not been given out, and he isn't expected back until next week.''

"Oh, I can wait.''

"Listen! I have a message for whoever might debark from the *Queen* and try calling him. That seems to be you, Donna Abrams. *Stay where you are.* Keep the door double-secured. Do not leave on any account. Do not admit anyone whatsoever, no matter what that person may claim, unless he gives you a password. When you hear it, be prepared to leave immediately. Do what you are told, and save your questions till later, when you're safe. Do you understand?''

"What? No, I don't. What's wrong?''

"I have not been informed.'' The lieutenant's mouth twisted into a smile. "But Sir Dominic is usually right about such things.''

Banner had met danger more than once. She had

always found it exhilarating. Her back straightened, her pulse slowed. Having repeated the instructions, she asked, "What's the password?"

"'Basingstoke.'" Okuma smiled again, wryly. "I don't know what it signifies. He has an odd sense of humor. Stand by. I've a call to make. Good luck." The screen darkened.

Banner started repacking.

The phone chimed.

The face she saw when she accepted was round and rubicund under yellow curls. "Dr. Abrams?" the man said. "Welcome to Terra. My name is Leighton, Tom Leighton, and I'm in the lobby. May I come up, or would you like to come down and join me?"

Again she sensed her aloneness. "Why?" she whispered.

"Well, I'm a colleague of yours. I've admired your work tremendously; those are classic presentations. By sheer chance, I was meeting a friend off the *Queen of Apollo* today, and he mentioned you'd been aboard. Believe me, it took detective work to track you down! Apparently you threw yourself into a cab and disappeared. I've had a data scan checking every hotel and airline and—Well, anyway, Dr. Abrams, I was hoping we could go out to dinner. My treat. I'd be honored."

She stared into the bland blue eyes. "Tell me," she said, "what do you think of the cater-cousin relationship among the Greech on Ramnu?"

"Huh?"

"Do you agree with me it's religious in origin, or do you think Brunamonti is right and it's a relic of the former military organization?"

"Oh, that! I agree with you absolutely."

"How interesting," Banner said, "in view of the fact that no such people as the Greech exist, that Ramnuans don't have religions of human type and

most definitely have never had armies, and nobody
named Brunamonti has ever done xenology on their

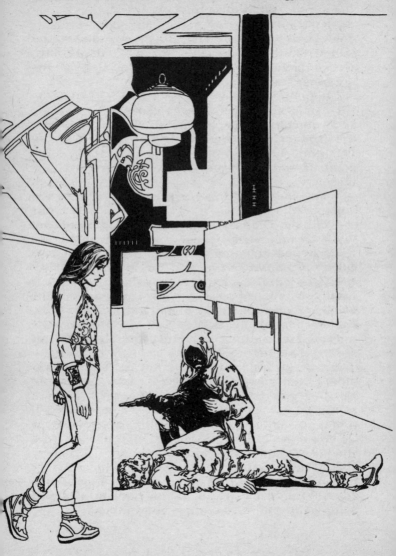

planet. Have you any further word for me, Citizen Leighton?"

"Ai, wait, wait a minute—"

She cut him off.

Presently her door was pealing. She punched the callbox and his voice came through: "Dr. Abrams, please, this is a terrible misunderstanding. Let me in and I'll explain."

"Go away." Despite the steadiness in her voice, her flesh crawled. She was concerned.

"Dr. Abrams, I must insist. The matter involves a very high-ranking person. If you don't open the door, we'll have to take measures."

"Or I will. Like calling the police."

"I tell you, it's a top-grade noble who wants to see you. He can have the police break you out of there. He'd rather not, because what he wants is for your benefit too, but—Uh, who are you?" Leighton asked somebody else. "What do you want?"

"*Basingstoke*," rippled a baritone voice. A moment later, Banner heard a thud. "You can open up now," the newcomer continued.

She did. Leighton lay in a huddle on the hall floor. Above him stood a figure in a hooded cloak. He drew the cowl back and she knew Flandry.

He gestured at the fallen shape. "A stun gun shot," he said. "I'll drag him in here to sleep it off. He's not worth killing, just a petty predator hired through an agency that provides reputable people with disreputable services. He's probably got a companion or two down below, on the *qui vive*. We'll spirit you upward. Chives—do you remember Chives?—has an aircar on the roof for us." He bowed and quickly, deftly kissed her hand. "I'm sorry about this informal reintroduction, my dear. I'll try to make amends at dinner. We have a reservation a couple of hours hence at Deirdre's. You wouldn't believe what they do with seafood there."

V

His Imperial Majesty, High Emperor Gerhart Siegmund Molitor, graciously agreed to withdraw from the reception for a private talk with its guest of honor. They passed in stateliness through the swirl of molten rainbows which several hundred costumes made of the grand ballroom. Folk bowed, curtsied, or saluted, depending on status, and hoped for a word from the august mouth. A few got one, and promptly became centers of eager attention. There were exceptions to this, of course, mostly older men of reserved demeanor, admirals, ministers of state, members of the Policy Board, the power brokers. Their stares followed the Duke of Hermes. He would be invited later to meet with various of them.

A gravshaft took Gerhart and Cairncross to a suite in the top of the loftiest tower that the Coral Palace boasted. The guards outside were not gorgeously uniformed like those on ground level; they were hard of face and hands, and their weapons had seen use. Gerhart motioned them not to follow, and let the door close behind himself and his companion.

A clear dome overlooked lower roofs, lesser spires, gardens, trianons, pools, bowers, finally beach, sand, surf, nearby residential rafts, and the Pacific Ocean. Sheening and billowing under a full Luna, those waters gave a sense of ancient forces still within this planet that man had so oedipally made his own, still biding their time. That feeling was strengthened by the sparsely furnished chamber. On the floor lay a rug made from the skin of a Germanian dolchzahn, on a desk stood a model of a corvette, things which had belonged to Hans. His picture hung on the wall. It had been taken seven years ago, shortly before his death, and Cairncross saw how wasted the big ugly countenance had become by then; but in caverns of bone, the gaze burned.

"Sit down," Gerhart said. "Smoke if you wish."

"I don't, but your Majesty is most kind."

Gerhart sighed. "Spare me the unction till we have to go back. When the lord of a fairly significant province arrives unannounced on Terra, I naturally look at whatever file we have on him. You don't strike me as the sort who would come here for a vacation."

"No, that was my cover story, . . . sir." The Emperor having taken a chair, the Duke did likewise.

"Ye-es," Gerhart murmured, "it is interesting that you put your head in the lion's mouth. Why?"

Cairncross regarded him closely. He didn't seem leonine, being of medium height, with blunt, jowly features and graying sandy hair. The iridescent, carefully draped robe he wore could not quite hide the fact that, in middle age, he was getting pudgy. But he had his father's eyes, small, dark, searching, the eyes of a wild boar.

He smiled as he opened a box and took out a cigar for himself. "Interesting enough," he went on, "that I've agreed to receive you like this. Ordinarily, you know, any special audiences you got would be with persons such as Intelligence officers."

"Frankly, sir," Cairncross answered, emboldened, "I started out that way, but got no satisfaction. Or so it appears. Maybe I'm doing the man an injustice. You can probably tell me — though Admiral Flandry is a devious devil, isn't he?"

"Flandry, eh? Hm-m." Gerhart kindled the cigar. Smoke curled blue and pungent. "Proceed."

"Sir," Cairncross began, "having seen my file, you know about the accusations and innuendos against me. I'm here partly to declare them false, to offer my body as a token of my loyalty. But you'll agree that more is needed, solid proof . . . not only to exonerate me, but to expose any actual plot."

"This is certainly an age of plots," Gerhart observed, through the same cold smile as before.

And murders, revolutions, betrayals, upheavals, Cairncross replied silently. *Brother against brother — When that spacecraft crashed, Gerhart, and killed Dietrich, was it really an accident? Incredible that safety routines could have slipped so far awry, for a ship which would carry the Emperor. Never mind what the board of inquiry reported afterward; the new Emperor kept tight control of its proceedings.*

You are widely believed to be a fratricide, Gerhart. (And a parricide? No; old Hans was too shrewd.) If you are nevertheless tolerated on the throne, it is because you are admittedly more able than dullard Dietrich was. The Empire needs a strong, skilled hand upon it, lest it splinter again in civil war and the Merseians or the barbarians return.

Yet that is your only claim to rulership, Gerhart. It was Hans' only claim, too. He, however, was coping as best he could, after the Wang dynasty fell apart. There was no truly legitimate heir. When most of the Navy rallied to him, he could offer domestic order and external security, at the cost of establishing a military dictatorship.

But . . . no blood of the Founder ever ran in his veins. His coronation was a solemn farce, played out under the watch of his Storm Corps, whose oath was not to the Imperium but to him alone. He broke aristocrats and made new ones at his pleasure. He kept no ancient pacts between Terra and her daughter worlds, unless they happened to suit his purposes. Law became nothing more than his solitary will.

He is of honored memory here, because of the peace he restored. That is not the case everywhere else. . . .

"You are suddenly very quiet," Gerhart said.

Cairncross started. "I beg your pardon, sir. I was thinking how to put my case with the least strain on your time and patience."

He cleared his throat and embarked on much the same discourse as he had given Flandry. The Emperor listened, watching him from behind a cloud of smoke.

Finally Gerhart nodded and said, "Yes, you are right. An investigation is definitely required. And it had better be discreet, or it would embarrass you politically—and therefore, indirectly, the Imperium." *If you are indeed loyal to us,* he left understood. "You ought to have instigated it earlier, in fact." *But a single planet is too huge, too diverse and mysterious, for anybody to rule wisely. As for an empire of planets —* "Now why do you insist that Vice Admiral Flandry take charge?"

"His reputation, sir," Cairncross declared. "He's accomplished fabulous things in the past when he had inadequate support or none. Who could better

handle our problem at Hermes, which includes the need not to bring in an army-sized team?"

Gerhart scowled. "You may have an exaggerated view of his abilities."

Yes, you don't like him, do you? Cairncross retorted inwardly. *He was your father's indispensable fox, he delivered a masterstroke at Chereion, and Dietrich relied on him too, occasionally. Rivalry; a living reminder of what you may prefer to forget; and, to be sure, I've learned in conversations with noblefolk, these last few days, that Flandry is apt to get flippant. He is not altogether reverent toward a crown that does not rest absolutely securely on a brow where it doesn't belong.*

"If so," he murmured, "then wouldn't a little demythologizing of him be welcome, sir?"

Gerhart stiffened in his chair. "By God—!"

"I don't imagine he would botch the assignment," Cairncross pursued. "He might perform brilliantly. He would at least be competent. But if he proved to be merely that—if, perhaps, a younger man had to come and take over—well, sir, it would be natural for you to do him the honor of relieving him of his duties yourself, with public thanks for past services."

Gerhart nodded hard. "Yes. Yes. High officers who've outlived their usefulness but can't be dismissed are always a nuisance. They've built their personal organizations, you see, and blocs of associates and admirers. . . . Well, Flandry. Since the middle of my father's reign, he has in effect been dreaming up his own assignments, and ruling over a tight-knit staff who report to nobody else. His conduct hasn't been insubordinate, but sometimes it has come close."

"I take your meaning, sir, after having dealt with him."

"What's happened?"

"Sir, I don't want to get above myself in the Imperial presence. Nevertheless, I am a ranking, governing noble of the Empire. Its welfare requires that its leaders get the respect they're entitled to. He didn't exactly refuse my commission, but he told me he'd have to think about whether or not he would condescend to accept it. After which he promptly disappeared on unspecified business, and is not expected back till next week. Meanwhile, I cool my heels."

Gerhart stroked his chin. "A direct order—putting him under your command—"

"Your Majesty is foresighted as well as generous."

Look met look in what Cairncross hoped Gerhart would assume was mutual understanding.

The guestroom door fluted. Banner jerked her head around. She had almost succeeded in losing herself in a starball game beamcast from Luna. At first she was attracted because she was a fan of several sports, and played when she could; but soon the ballet-like, dreamlike beauty of the motion took her. Now abruptly it was unreal, against the leap in her pulse and the dryness in her mouth.

Angered by that, she told herself to calm down and act like an adult. Aloud, she asked, "Who is it, please?"

There should be no danger. Flandry had decided his place right in Archopolis was probably her safest hideaway. He could smuggle her in; Chives, in constant electronic touch with his immediate juniors, could fend off any visitors while the admiral was away.

He had been gone for two achingly idle days. She felt more relief than was rational to hear his voice: "The gentleman from Basingstoke. Come on out, if you will. I bear tidings."

"A, a minute, please." She'd been basking under a sunlamp, after a lengthy swim, while she watched the contest. He had not so much as hinted at a pass. Mostly, in what little conversation they'd held on personal topics, he reminisced about her father and drew forth her own memories of his old mentor. Besides, mores were casual on Terra. Nevertheless, she didn't want to meet him unclad. She scrambled into slacks, blouse, sandals. Only after she was through the door did she remember that she hadn't stopped to brush her hair and it must look like two comets colliding.

He didn't appear to notice, though she suspected he did. He himself wore inconspicuous civilian garb. His expression was grim. "How've you been?" he asked.

"In suspense," she admitted. "And you?"

"Skulking, but busy. I had to keep out of sight, you see, to maintain the pretense that I'd never returned here. At the same time, I had to learn what's been going on; and my people are as wary as anyone could want, but I dared not simply ring them up and inquire." He shrugged. "Details. I managed. Let's have a drink while I bring you *au courant*."

She didn't recognize that expression. Her knowledge of non-Anglic human languages was limited, and fresh only as regarded terms in the Oriental classics that, translated, she enjoyed. She understood him in context, however, and followed him eagerly. As a rule she was a light drinker, her vice was tobacco, but in this hour she desired a large cognac.

Rain washed silvery down the outer side of the living room, which had been left transparent. Often lightning flashed. She heard no thunder through the soundproofing, and that made the whole scene feel eerily unreal. They settled into loungers opposite each other, amidst soft-colored drapes whose textures were meant to be touched, art from a dozen worlds, a drift of incense. Chives heard their wishes and departed. They lit cigarettes.

"Well?" Banner demanded. "Speak up. . . . I'm sorry, I didn't mean to bark at you."

"Would you care for some nerve soother?"

She shook her head. "Just the drink. I—In my line

of work, we dare not use much chemical calming. The temptation could get too great—no addiction, of course, but the temptation."

He nodded and said low, "Yes, you've suffered a lot of tension and pain, as well as excitement, vicariously, haven't you?"

"Vicariously? No! It's as real for me as it's been for Yewwl!" Banner was surprised at her vehemence. She quenched it. "I'll try to explain later, if we have a chance."

"Oh, we ought to have that," Flandry said. "We're off together for Ramnu."

"What?" She stared.

Chives brought the drinks. Flandry's was beer. He savored a long swallow. "Aaah." He smiled. "You know, that's among the things I miss the most on an extended job. Hard liquor can be carried along in ample supply, or can usually be found if a person isn't fussy, but dear old beer doesn't tolerate concentration and reconstitution as certain people who lack taste buds believe, and it has too much volume for more than a few cases to go aboard *Hooligan*." He inhaled above the goblet. "Gather ye bubbles while ye may."

"Do you always joke?" she wondered.

He shrugged again. "Might as well. The grief will take care of itself, never fear." His mouth fell into harsh curves, his gray eyes locked onto hers. "All right, I'll get serious. To begin, what understanding of the situation do you have?"

"Hardly any, for certain," she reminded him. "I've made my guesses, and told you them, but you were, oh, noncommittal."

"I'd too few facts," he explained, "and empty speculation is worse than a waste of time, it's apt to mislead. Actually, for a person who's been sheltered from the nastier facts of political life, you made a pretty canny surmise or two. But maybe I'd best retrace everything from my viewpoint."

He wet his throat afresh, filled his lungs, and proceeded: "It appeared plausible, from your account, that Cairncross is conducting business that he doesn't care to reveal before he's ready. If it doesn't center at Ramnu, at least Ramnu is critical to it. Several years ago, he replaced the management of the commercial Hermetian enterprise there. Since, it's expanded operations, but at the same time grown remarkably tight-lipped. It also gives your scientific outfit less and less cooperation. The pretexts are not convincing. This hampers your work, restricts its scope, and may at last choke it off altogether.

"Meanwhile, Cairncross has declined to consider rehabilitating Ramnu. He might reasonably maintain it's too expensive for his budget. But why wouldn't he pass your appeal on to Terra? His rank is sufficient that he'd have a fair chance of getting approval; nowadays the Policy Board likes to start worthy projects, if they don't cost a lot, to help build goodwill for an Imperium that badly needs it. The influx of technicians and money, the stimulus given local industries, would benefit a Hermetian economy that is not in ideal shape at present.

"Well, you decided to invoke my influence, for old times' sake. Your idea of its magnitude was unrealistic, but you couldn't know that. You could at least have persuaded me to go look the place over, and see if I couldn't invent a lever that would pry authorization loose from the Board.

"Before your liner could reach Terra, Cairncross arrived personally in a speedster. He wanted me to flit home with him immediately. Coincidence? He is in fact getting a bad name in some limited Imperial circles. No bad enough to provoke action by our lumbering, creaky, half-programmed Empire, but still—Nevertheless, why insist on me handling his chestnuts, and no one else? Why so stiffly opposed to traveling in leisure and comfort on the *Queen?* Could it be that somebody was bound here aboard her, somebody he'd prefer I not meet?

"You may remember how I inquired at tedious length about what went on at your host's place in Starfall, including the layout of the house. You'd taken precautions. But neither you nor yonder Citizen Runeberg is a professional in that field. I can think of a thousand ways to eavesdrop on you."

Flandry stopped and drained his beer. "Chives!" he bawled. "More!" To Banner: "I require a pitcher of this whenever I lecture on my trade, which is twice a year at the Corps Academy. Excuse me if I've droned on. Professoring is a habit that gets hard to break."

She comforted her body with cognac. "No, you've done right," she whispered. "That is, most of it had become fairly clear to me, but you've put it in perspective."

"The rest is more briefly told. For small blessings, give thanks," he said. Chives brought a fresh goblet, glanced at how Banner was doing, and withdrew.

"You made an excuse to delay matters," she said, to demonstrate that she was not lost. "This required you drop out of sight till after the *Queen* had left Terra, as if you gave her no more thought. But you alerted your staff."

"On a basis of guesswork. I had scant notion of who, or what, if anything, would arrive, or even if that arrival would concern me. It was merely a contingency that needed to be covered. If nothing had come of it, I'd have used the time to think of more contingencies and try to provide against them. As was, I played by ear. It seems likely that Cairncross engaged agents to head you off, but I can't prove it. No use carting away the one I clobbered, for a quiz. He wouldn't have known. His bosses are professionals too."

"What have you done since?"

"Research, and assorted preparation-making, and—Yesterday, checking with this office, I found it had received a direct Imperial order placing me under the Duke's command, to report to him without delay and be prepared to depart for Hermes pronto if not sooner." Flandry's grin was vulpine. "Since it's clear that I would not break contact with my staff, I couldn't stay away on plea of ignorance. As an experiment, I requested an audience with his Majesty, and was quite unsurprised to be told that no time will be available for me until next month."

He sipped. "Therefore I've returned like a nice boy," he said. "His Grace was equally nice. If he thinks I may have had a part in the sudden sleepiness of that agent and in your disappearance, he didn't let on. And perhaps he doesn't. A heavy stun gun blast has an amnesiac effect on the preceding few hours, you know. For all that chap can tell, you admitted him and shot him yourself before you fled. The Duke knows how leery of him you are, and that you've spent many years partaking in a violent milieu. One thing I have ascertained is that he's put the rent-a-thug organization on a full-scale hunt for you. But in any event, he was glad to learn I can leave tomorrow early." He winced. "Exceedingly early."

Dismay smote. "But what shall I do?" Banner asked.

"The plan, such as it is, is this," Flandry told her. "I've explained that it's best I go in my own speedster. She's equipped for field work, you see. I can commence in a preliminary way as soon as I reach Hermes. She doesn't have room for him and his entourage—polite word for bodyguards, plus an aide or two and perhaps a mistress—but his craft is nearly as fast.

"Once there . . . well, he'll suppose, maybe I can

be won over. Surely I can be stalled, bogged down, put on false scents, possibly hoodwinked altogether. If not, I can be made to die. My distinct impression is that his Grace doesn't need much longer to launch his scheme. Else he wouldn't be acting this boldly; he's too committed by now to dare be timid."

"Can't you tell anyone?" she breathed.

"Oh, yes, if I want to endanger those persons needlessly," he answered. "For what could an underling do? I've left a record of what I think, keyed into a computer, which will release it to selected individuals upon my death or prolonged vanishment. A gesture, mostly, I'm afraid. After all, thus far it amounts to scarcely more than conjecture; no firm evidence. Besides, my insubordination will gravely discredit it."

"In . . . insubordination?" Her scalp tingled.

He nodded. "Yes. I won't be steering for Hermes but for Ramnu. That is, if you'll come along as my absolutely necessary guide. Ramnu's apparently a vulnerable flank that he may or may not have covered well enough—probably not, since he's so anxious to keep me from it. We might discover what we need to discover, though time will be damnably short. If we fail, or if it turns out there really is nothing amiss—then we're liable to charges of treason, having disobeyed an order of the very Emperor, and they will certainly be brought."

His smooth manner was gone; he looked miserable. "I've committed my share of evil, in line of work," he said. "Inviting a daughter of Max Abrams to accompany me may be the worst of the lot. I hope you'll have the sense to refuse."

It blazed in her. She sprang to her feet. "Of course I don't!" she cried, and lifted her glass on high.

Lightning glared. The rainstorm grew more wild.

VI

———————◆———————

Hooligan raised her lean form off the spacefield and hit the sky as fast as regulations allowed. Thunder trailed. Beyond atmosphere, she curved away as per flight plan, accelerating harder all the time. Presently she was far enough distant from regular traffic trajectories that she could unbind the full power of her gravs. Before long, Terra was visibly dwindling in eyesight, more quickly for each second that passed.

None of this was felt inboard, where fields maintained a steady one gee of weight. Only the faintest susurrus resounded, and most of that was from the ventilators which kept vernal breezes moving. *Hooligan* was a deceptive craft: small, but overpowered, with armament to match a corvette's, equipment and data banks to match an explorer's (and an Intelligence laboratory's), luxury to match— but here Banner's experience failed her.

In her stateroom, which gave on a private bath cubicle, she removed her disguise. It came off easier than she had expected, not just the dress and wig

but the items which had altered her looks and prints to fit the passport Flandry had given her.

Sarah Pipelini — "Is this anybody real?" she had asked.

"Well, several real persons have found it convenient to be her for a while," he replied. "She's got the standard entries in official records, birth, education, residence, employment, et cetera, plus occasional changes to stay plausible. I've a number of identities available. Sarah's is the easiest to suit you to. Besides, creating her was fun."

"I'm no good at playacting," Banner said nervously. "It's too short notice even to learn what her past life is supposed to have been."

"No need. Simply memorize what's in the passport. Stay close to me and don't speak unless spoken to. No harm if you register excitement; that's natural, when you're off on a trip to far-off, exotic Hermes. It'll also be natural for you to clutch my arm and give me intermittent adoring glances, if you can bring yourself to that."

"You mean — ?"

"Why, I thought it was obvious. We have to get you aboard. Besides the regular Naval clearance procedures, Cairncross will doubtless have agents unobtrusively watching. No surprise if I bring a lady along to help pass the time of voyage. In fact, that will reinforce the impression — together with just Chives coming otherwise — that I am indeed going where I'm supposed to. If I brought any of my staff, then his Grace might well demand that men of his be included. As is, I've already filed our list, the three of us, you described as a 'friend.' Cairncross may snigger when he reads it, but he should believe." Flandry's tone grew serious. "Of course, this is strictly a ruse. Have no fears."

When he applied the deceptive materials, her face had burned beneath his fingers.

Now she showered the sweat of tension off her. For a moment she regarded her rangy form in the mirror and considered putting the glamorous gown on again. But once more she flushed, and chose the plainest coverall she had packed. She did brush her hair till it shone and let it flow free under a head-band of lovely weave.

Emerging, she found the saloon where Flandry had said they would meet, and drew a quick breath. She had often seen open space, through a faceplate as well as a viewscreen. Yet somehow, at this instant, those star-fires crowding yonder clear blackness, that icy sweep of the galaxy, and Terra already a blue jewel falling away into depths beyond depths—reached in and seized her.

Music drew her back. A lilt of horns, flutes, violins . . . Mozart? Flandry entered. He too had changed clothes, his uniform for an open-necked bouffalon shirt, bell-bottomed slacks, curly-toed slippers. *Is he being casual on my account?* she wondered. *If so, he still can't help being elegant. The way he bears his head, and the light makes its gray come alive—*

"How're you doing?" he greeted. "Relaxed, I trust? You may as well be. We've a good two weeks' travel before us." He grinned. "At least, I hope we can make them good."

"Won't we have work to do?" she inquired hastily.

"Oh, the ship conns herself *en route*, and handles other routine like housekeeping. Chives handles the meals, which, believe me, will not be routine. He promises lunch in an hour." Flandry gestured at a table of dark-red wood—actual mahogany? Banner had seen literary references to mahogany. "Let's have an apéritif meanwhile."

"But, but you admitted you know almost nothing about Ramnu. I'm sure you've loaded the data banks with information on it, but won't you need a lot of that in your mind, also?"

He guided her by the elbow to a padded bench that curved around three sides of the table. Above it, on a bulkhead that shimmered slightly iridescent, was screened a picture she recognized: snowscape, three trudging peasants, a row of primitive houses, winter-bare trees, a mountain, all matching the grace of the music. Hiroshige had wrought it, twelve hundred years ago.

"Please sit," he urged. They did. "My dear," he continued, "of course I'll have to work. We both will. But I'm a quick study; and what's the use of laying elaborate plans when most of the facts are unknown? We'll do best to enjoy yourselves while we can. For openers, you need a day off to learn, down in your bones, that for the nonce you're *safe*." Chives appeared. "What will you drink? Since I understand a seafood salad is in preparation, I'd recommend a dry white wine."

"Specifically, sir, the Château Huon '58," said the Shalmuan.

Flandry raised his brows. "A pinot noir blanc?"

"The salad will be based upon Unan Besarian skimmerfish, sir."

Flandry stroked his mustache. "I see. Then when we eat, we'll probably want—oh, never mind, you'll pick the bottle anyway. Very good, Chives."

The servant left, waving his tail. Banner sighed. "Where can you possibly find time for gourmandizing, Admiral?" she asked.

"Why, isn't that the purpose of self-abnegation, to gain the means of self-indulgence?" Flandry chuckled. "I'd prefer to be a decadent aristocrat, but wasn't born to it; I've had to earn my decadence."

"I can't believe that," she challenged.

"Well, at any rate, frankly, you strike me as being too earnest. Your father knew how to savor the cosmos, in his gusty fashion. So did your mother, in her quieter way, and I daresay she does yet. Why not you?"

"Oh, I do. It's simply that—" Banner stared past him, into brilliance and darkness. She wasn't given to revealing herself, especially on acquaintance as brief as this. However, Flandry was an old family friend, and they'd be together in running between the claws of death, and—and—

"I never had a chance to learn much about conventional pleasures," she explained with difficulty. "Navy brat, you know, shunted from planet to planet, educated mostly by machines. Then the Academy; I had an idea of enlisting in Dad's corps—yours—and a xenological background would help. But I got into the science entirely, instead, and left for Ramnu, and that's where I've been ever since." She met his eyes. They were kindly. "I wouldn't want it any different, either," she said. "I have the great good fortune to love what I do . . . and those I do it with, the Ramnuans themselves."

He nodded. "I can see how it would make you its own. Nothing less than total dedication will serve, will it? On a world so strange." His vision likewise sought the deeps outside. "Gods of mystery," he whispered, "it wasn't supposed to be possible, was it? A planet like that. Yes, I do have a brain-scorching lot of homework ahead of me. To start off, I don't even know how Ramnu is supposed to have happened."

Originally a dwarf sun had a superjovian attendant, a globe of some 3000 Terrestrial masses. Such a monster was, inevitably, of starlike composition, mainly hydrogen, with a small percentage of helium, other elements a mere dash of impurities.

Indeed, it must have been more nearly comparable to a star than to, say, Jupiter. The latter is primarily liquid, beneath a vast atmosphere; a slag of light metal compounds does float about in

continent-sized pieces, but most solid material is at the core (if it can be called solid, under that pressure). The slow downdrift of matter, drawn by the gravity of the stupendous mass, releases energy; Jupiter radiates about twice what it receives from Sol, making the surface warm.

Increase the size by a factor of 10, and everything changes. The body glows red; it is liquid, or fiercely compressed gas, throughout, save that the heavy elements which have sunken to the center are squeezed into quantum degeneracy, rigid beyond any stuff we will ever hold in our hands. At the same time, because its gravitational grip upon itself is immense, a globe like this can form, and can survive, rather close to an ordinary sun. Energy input from light and solar wind is insufficient to blow molecules away from it.

Unless—

Close by, as astronomical distances go, was a giant star. It went supernova. This may have occurred by chance, when it was passing precisely far enough away. Likelier, giant and dwarf were companions, with precisely the right orbits around each other. In the second case, the catastrophe tore them apart, for mass was lost at such a rate that conservation of momentum whirled the pair off at greater than escape velocity.

A violence that briefly rivalled the combined output of billions of suns did more than this. It filled surrounding space with gas that, for millennia afterward, made a nebula visible across light-years, till at last expansion thinned it away into the abyss. The dwarf star may well have captured a little of that cloud, and moved up the main sequence.

The huge planet was too small for that; parameters were wrong for producing another Mirkheim. Bombardment and sheer incandescence blew away more than 90 percent of it, the hydrogen and helium. They volatilized mainly as a plasma, which interacted with the core of heavier elements through magnetic fields. Thus the rotation of that core was drastically slowed. It exploded too, out of super-compaction into a state we might call normal. This outburst was insufficient to shatter the remnant, though perhaps a fraction was lost. But the ball of silicon, nickel, iron, carbon, oxygen, nitrogen, uranium . . . was molten for eons afterward.

Meanwhile, its lesser satellites, like its lesser sister planets, had been vaporized. A part of three big ones survived. The shrinkage of their primary sent them spiraling outward to new orbits. Movement was hindered by friction with the nebula, which was substantial for thousands of years. That may have caused an inner moon or two to crash on the planet. Certainly it moved the globe itself sunward.

When finally things had stabilized, there was Niku, a late G-type star of 0.48 Solar luminosity, unusual only in having a higher percentage of metals than is common for bodies its age (and this only if we have estimated that age correctly). There were four small, virtually airless planets. And there was Ramnu, circling Niku at a mean distance, which varied little, of 1.10 astronomical unit, in a period of 1.28 standard year. Its mass was 310 times the Terrestrial, its mean density 1.1 times —but the density was due to self-compression under 7.2 standard gees, for the overall compositions were similar. The axial tilt of Ramnu was about 4 degrees, its rotation period equal to 15.7 standard days.

As the stone cooled, it outgassed, forming oceans and a primordial atmosphere. Chemical evolution began. Eventually photosynthesizing life developed, and the pace of that evolution quickened. Today the atmosphere resembled Terra's, apart from slight differences in proportions of constituents. The most striking unlikeness was its con-

centration, 4.68 times the Terrestrial at sea level,
which meant 33.7 times the pressure. Thus, although irradiation from the sun was 0.4 what Terra
gets, greenhouse effect kept the surface reasonably
warm . . . but this fluctuated.

The world was discovered not by humans but by
Cynthians, early in the pioneering era. Intrigued,
they established a scientific base on its innermost
moon and bestowed names from a mythology of
theirs. Politico-economic factors, which also fluc-
tuate, soon caused them to depart. Later, humans
arrived, intending to stay and operate on a larger
scale. But the facilities made available to them were
never adequate, and lessened across the centuries.
For all its uniqueness, Ramnu remained obscure,
even among planetologists.

There are so many, many worlds, in this tiny seg-
ment of space we have somewhat explored.

When safely high in Sol's potential well, *Hooligan*
switched to secondary drive. Her oscillators gave
her a pseudovelocity almost twice that of most vessels, better than half a light-year per hour. Yet she
would take half a month to reach the region of Sol's
near neighbor Antares. Had she been able to range
that far, it would have taken her twenty years to
cross the galaxy. Their compensators cancelling the
optical effects of continuous spatial displacement,
her screens showed heaven slowly changing, as old
constellations became new; unless made to amplify,
on the fourth day they no longer showed Sol.

"Which shows you how we rate in the scheme of
things, doesn't it?" Flandry said apropos. He and
Banner were relaxing over drinks after she had led
him through a hard session of study. The drinks
now totalled several.

She leaned elbows on the table and gave him a
serious regard. "Depends on what you mean by

that," she replied. "If God can care about the workmanship in an electron, He can care about us."

He looked back. It was worth doing, he thought. She wasn't beautiful by conventional measures, but her face had good bones and was more alive than most—like her springy body and those leaf-green, sea-green eyes. . . . "I didn't know you were religious," he said. "Well, Max was, though he made no production of it."

"I'm not sure if I'd call myself religious," she admitted. "I'm not observant in any faith. But Creation must have a purpose."

He sipped his Scotch and followed the smoke-bite with a little water. "The present moment could make me believe that," he said. "Unfortunately, I've seen too many moments which are not the least like it. I don't find much self-created purpose in our lives, either. And our public creations, like the Empire, are exercises in absurdity." He took forth his cigarette case. "Ah, well, we went through this argument at the age of eighteen or thereabouts, didn't we? Smoke?"

She accepted, and they kindled together. He had selected for music a concert by an ensemble of tuned Freyan ornithoids. They twittered, they trilled, they sang of treetops and twilit skies. He had given the air a greenwood odor and made it summer-mild. The lights were low.

Banner seemed abruptly to have forgotten her surroundings. She inhaled as sharply as her gaze focused on him. "Did you?" she asked. "At just about that age, weren't you serving the Empire . . . under my father? And afterward, everything you've done—No, don't bother playing your cynicism game with me."

He shrugged and laughed. "*Touché!* I confess I matured a trifle late. Max was a stout Imperial loyalist, of course, and I admired him more than any other man I've ever met, including the one alleged to have been my own father. So it took me a while to see what the Empire really is. Since then, if you must know, like everybody else who can think, I have indeed been playing games, for lack of better occupation. Mine happen to be useful to Terra—and, to be sure, to myself, since our pre-eminence is more fun than subjugation, barbarism, or death. But as for taking the Imperial farce seriously—"

He stopped, seeing appalled anger upon her. "Do you say my father was a fool?" cracked forth.

Am I drunk? flashed through him. *A bit, maybe, what with alcohol poured straight over weariness and, yes, loneliness. I ought to have been more careful.*

"I'm sorry, Banner," he apologized. "I spoke heedlessly. No, your father was right at the time. The Empire was worth something then, on balance. Afterward, well, from his standpoint it doubtless continued to be. If he grew disappointed, he would have felt obliged to keep silent. He was that kind of man. I like to imagine that he lived and died in the hope of a renascence—which I wish I could share."

Her countenance softened. "You don't?" she murmured. "But why? The Empire keeps the Pax, holds the trade lanes open, fends off the outside enemy, guards the heritage—*That's* what you've spent your life doing."

Aye, she remains her father's daughter, he saw. *It explains much about her.*

"Excuse me," he said. "I was being grumpy."

"No, you weren't," she declared. "I may not be a very skilled human-reader, but you meant your words. Unmistakably. Please tell me more."

Her spirit is bent to the search for truth.

"Oh, it's a long story and a longer thesis," he said. "The Empire had value once. It still does, to a degree. Nevertheless, what was it ever in the first place, but the quickest and crudest remedy for chaos? And what brought on the chaos, the Troubles, except the suicide of an earlier order, which couldn't muster the will to keep freedom alive? So again, as before, came Caesar.

"But a universal state is not a new beginning for a civilization, it's the start of the death, and it has to follow the same course over and over through history, like a kind of slow but terminal sickness."

He sipped, he smoked, feeling the slight burns of each. "I'd really rather not give you a lecture tonight," he said. "I've spent hundreds of hours when I'd nothing else to do, reading and meditating; and I've talked to historians, psychodynamicists, philosophers; yes, nonhuman observers of us have had cogent remarks to make—But the point is simply that you and I happen to be living in a critical stage of the Empire's decline, the interregnum between its principate and dominate phases."

"You *are* getting abstract," Banner said.

Flandry smiled. "Then let's drop the subject and watch it squash. Chives will clean up the mess."

She shook her head. Subtle shadows went over the curves around cheekbones and jawline. "No, please, not like that. Dominic—Admiral, I'm not entirely ignorant. I know about corruption and abuse of power, not to mention civil wars or plain stupidity. My father used to do some wonderful cursing, when a piece of particularly nauseous news came in. But he'd always tell me not to expect perfection of mortal beings; our duty was to keep on trying."

He didn't remark on her use of his first name, though his heart did. "I suppose that's forever true, but it's not forever possible," he responded gravely. "Once as a young fellow I found myself supporting the abominable Josip against McCormac— Remember McCormac's Rebellion? He was infinitely the better man. Anybody would have been.

But Josip was the legitimate Emperor, and legitimacy is the root and branch of government. How else, in spite of the cruelties and extortions and ghastly mistakes it's bound to perpetrate—how else, by what right, can it command loyalty? If it is not the servant of Law, then it is nothing but a temporary convenience at best. At worst, it's raw force.

"And this is where we are today. Hans Molitor did his damnedest to restore the old institutions, which is why I did my damnedest for him. But we were too late. They'd been perverted too much for too long; too little faith in them remained. Now nobody can claim power by right—only by strength. Fear makes the rulers ever more oppressive, which provokes ever more unhappiness with them, which rouses dreams in the ambitious—"

He slapped the tabletop. "No, I do not like the tone of this conversation!" he exclaimed. "Can't we discuss something cheerful? Tell me about Ramnuan funeral customs."

She touched his hand. "Yes. Give me one word more, only one, and we'll see if we can't ease off. You're right, Dad never gave up hope. Have you, really?"

"Oh, no," he said with a smile and a dram of sincerity. "The sophont races will survive. In due course, they'll build fascinating new civilizations. Cultures of mixed species look especially promising. Consider Avalon already."

"I mean for us," she insisted. "Our children and grandchildren."

Do you still think of having children, Banner? "There too," Flandry told her. "That is, I'm not optimistic about this period we're in; but it can be made less terrible than it'd otherwise be. And that isn't so little, is it—buying years for billions of sentient beings, that they can live in? But it'll not be easy."

"Which is why you're bound where you are," she said low. Her eyes lingered upon him.

"And you, my dear. And good old Chives." He stubbed out his cigarette. "Now you've had your answer, such as it is, and I demand my turn. I want to discourse on anything else, preferably trivial. Or what say we play dance music and try a few steps? Else I'll grow downright eager to study onward about our destination."

Because of its gravity, which prevents the rise of very high lands, and because of the enormous out-welling of water from its interior, Ramnu has pro-portionately less dry surface than Terra. However, what it does have equals about 20 times the Terran, and some of the continents are Eurasia-sized. There are many islands.

Its surviving moons, what is left of them, are still of respectable mass: Diris, 1.69 Luna's; Tiglaia, 4.45; Elaveli, 6.86, comparable to Ganymede. But only the first is close enough to have a significant tidal effect, and that is small and moves creepingly. Niku's pull is slightly more. The oceans are less salty than Terra's, with far less in the way of currents.

The weakness of the tides is partially offset by the weight and speed of ocean waves. Winds, slow but ponderous, raise great rollers across those immen-sities, which reach shore with crushing power. Hence sea cliffs and fjords are rare. Coasts are usu-ally jumbles of rock, or long beaches, or brackish marshes.

Mountains are farther apart on the average than on Terra, and the tallest stands a mere 1500 meters. (There the steep pressure gradient has reduced air pressure to one-fourth its sea-level value.) Elevated areas do tend to spread more widely than on Terra, because of heavier erosion carrying material down from the heights as well as because of stronger

forces raising them. In the working of those forces, plumes are more important than plate movement. Thus much landscape consists of hills or of high plains, carved and scored by wind, water, frost, creep, and similar action of the planet. Volcanoes are abundant and, while uplands are rapidly worn away, elsewhere new ones are always being lifted.

Given the thick atmosphere, small Coriolis force, and comparatively low irradiation, cyclonic winds are weak and cyclonic storms very rare. The boiling point of water, about 241° C. at sea level, also has a profound effect on meteorology. Moisture comes more commonly as mist than as rain or snow, making haziness normal. Once formed in the quickly thinning upper air, clouds tend to be long-lived and to make overcasts. Above them, the sky is often full of ice crystals. When precipitation does occur, it is apt to be violent, and to bring radical changes in the weather.

Atmospheric circulation is dominated by two basic motions. First is the flow of cold air from the poles toward the equator, forcing warmer air aloft and poleward—Hadley cells. Second is the horizontal flow engendered by the temperature differential between day and night sides. Consequently, tropical winds tend to blow against the sun; the winds of the temperate zones generally have an equatorward slant; and storms are everywhere frequent about dawn and sunset, this being when precipitation is likeliest. In higher latitudes, cold fronts often collide, with impressive results. As observed before, though winds are slow by Terran standards, *ceteris paribus*, they push hard.

Even during interglacial periods, the polar caps are extensive; having fallen there frozen, water does not readily rise again. Moreover, the circulation patterns of air and water combine with the slight axial tilt to make for much greater dependence of climate on latitude alone than is true of terrestroid worlds. Because of that same axial tilt, plus the nearly circular orbit, there are no real seasons on Ramnu. The basic cycle is not of the year but of the half-month-long day.

Across it strides another cycle, irregular, millennial, and vast—that of the glaciers. Given its overall chilliness, its extensive cloud decks, and its reluctance to let water evaporate, Ramnu is always close to the brink of an ice age, or else over it. No more is necessary than the upthrust of a new highland in a high latitude. Accompanied as it is by massive vulcanism, which fills the upper atmosphere with dust that will be decades in settling, this makes snow fall; and given the pressure gradient, the snow line is low. The ice spreads outward and outward, sometimes through a single hemisphere, sometimes through both. Nothing stops it but the subtropical belts. Nothing makes it retreat but the sinking of the upland that formed it.

For the past billion years or more, Ramnu had alternated between glacial and interglacial periods. The former usually prevailed longer. Humans arrived when the ice was again on the march. Now it was advancing at terrible speed, kilometers each year. Whole ecologies withered before it. Native cultures fled or crumbled—as how many times before in unrecorded ages?

Banner sought help for them. A starfaring civilization could readily provide that. Intensive studies would be needed at first, of course, followed by research and development, but the answer was simple in principle. Orbit giant solar mirrors in the right sizes and numbers and paths, equipped with sensors, computers, and regulators so that they would continuously adjust their orientations to the optimum for a given set of conditions. Have them send down the right amounts of extra warmth to

properly chosen regions. That was all. The glaciers would crawl back to the poles where they belonged, and never return.

Banner sought help. The Grand Duke of Hermes placed himself squarely in her way. Flandry could guess why.

Hooligan contained a miniature gymnasium. Her captain and passenger took to using it daily after work, together. Then they would return to their cabins, wash, dress well, and meet for cocktails before dinner.

In a certain watch, about mid-passage, they were playing handball. The sphere sprang between them, caromed off bulkheads, whizzed through space, smacked against palms, flew opponentward followed and met by laughter. Bare feet knew the springiness of deck covering, the jubilation of upward flight. Sweat ran down skin and across lips with a rousing sting of salt. Lungs drew deep, hearts drummed, blood coursed.

She was ahead by a few points, but it hadn't been easy and she was not a bit sure it would last. Seventeen years made amazingly little difference. He was nearly as fast and enduring as a youth.

And nearly as slim and supple, she saw. Above and below his shorts, under smooth brown skin, muscles went surging, not heavy but long, lively, greyhound and race horse muscles. Wetness made him gleam. He grinned at her, flash after white flash in those features that time had not blurred, simply whetted. She realized he was enjoying the sight of her in turn, more than he was the game. The knowledge tingled.

He took the ball, whirled on his heel, and sped it aside. Before it had rebounded, he was running to intercept. She was too. They collided. In a ridiculous tangle of limbs, they fell.

He raised himself to his knees. "Banner, are you all right?" As she regained her breath, she heard anxiety in his tone. Looking up, she saw it in his face.

"Yes," she mumbled. "Just had the wind knocked out of me."

"Are you sure? I'm bloody sorry. Both my left feet must've been screwed on backwards this morning."

"Oh, not your fault, Dominic. Not any more than mine. I'm all right, really I am. Are you?" She sat up.

It brought them again in close contact, thighs, arms, a breast touching him. She felt his warmth and sweat through the halter. The clean man-smell enfolded her, entered her. Their lips were centimeters apart. *I'd better rise, fast,* she thought in a distant realm, but couldn't. Their eyes were holding too hard. As if of themselves, hers closed partway, while her mouth barely opened.

The kiss lasted for minutes of sweetness and lightning.

When he reached below the halter, alarm shrilled her awake. She disengaged her face and pushed at his chest. "No, Dominic," she heard herself say. It wavered. "No, please."

If he insists, she knew, *I won't.* And she did not know what she felt, or was supposed to feel, when he immediately let go.

He sprang to his feet and offered his assistance. They stood for a moment and looked. Finally he smiled in his wry fashion.

"I won't say I'm sorry, because I don't want to lie to you," he told her. "It was delightful. But I do beg your pardon."

She managed a shaken laugh. "I'm not sorry either, and no pardon is called for. We both did that."

"Then—" He half reached for her, before his arm dropped. "Have no fears," he said gently. "I can mind my manners. I've done it in the past . . . yes, right here."

How many women has he traveled with? How few have denied him?

If only I can make him understand. If only I do myself.

She knotted her fists, swallowed twice, and forced out: "Dominic, listen. You're a damned attractive man, and I'm no timid virgin. But I, I'm not wanton either."

"No," he said, with utmost gravity, "the daughter of Max and Marta wouldn't be. I forgot myself. It won't happen again."

"I told you, I forgot too!" she cried. "Or—well, I w-wish we knew each other better."

"I hope we will. As friends, whether or not you ever feel like more than that. Shake on it?"

Tears blurred the sight of him as they clasped hands. She blinked them off her lashes, vexedly. Too fast for her to stop it, her voice blurted, "Oh, hell, if I had a normal sex drive we'd be down on the deck yet!"

He cocked his head. "You mean you don't? I decline to believe that." In haste: "Not that it'd be any disgrace. Nobody is strong in every department, and no single department is at the core of life. But I think you're mistaken. The cause is easy to see."

She stared at her toes. "I've not had much to do . . . there . . . ever . . . nor missed it much."

"Same cause. You've been too thoroughly directed toward the nonhuman." He laid a hand on her shoulders. "That's not wrong. In many ways, it's wonderful. But it has given your emotions different expression from what's customary, and I think that in turn has made you a bit confused about them. Not to worry, dear."

All at once her face was buried against him, and he was holding her around the waist and stroking her hair and murmuring.

Presently she could stand back. "Would you like to talk about it?" he asked. With a disarming chuckle: "I'll bend a sympathetic ear, but it'll also be a fascinated one. What *is* it like, to share the life of an alien . . . to be an alien?"

"Oh, no, you exaggerate," she said. Relief billowed through her. *Yes, I do want to talk about what matters to me. I can't just go take a shower as if nothing had happened, I have to let out this fire. He's shown me I needn't be afraid to, because the talk needn't be about us.* "It's basically nothing but a wide-band communication link, you know."

(The collar that Yewwl wore was a piece of electronic sorcery. A television scanner saw in the same direction as her eyes. An audio pickup heard what she did. Thermocouples, vibrosensors, chemosensors analyzed their surroundings to get at least a clue to what she felt, smelled, tasted. The whole of the result became more than the sum of the parts, after it reached Banner.

(It did that by radio, at the highest frequencies to which Ramnu's air was transparent. A well-shielded gram of radioisotope sufficed to power a signal that human-made comsats could detect and relay. A specialized computer in Wainwright Station received the signals and converted them back to sensory-like data. The ultimate translation, though, had to be by a human, brain and body alike, intellect, imagination, empathy developed through year after year. Seated beneath the helmet, before the video screen, hands flat on a pair of subtly vibrant plates, Banner could almost—almost—submerge herself in her oath-sister.

(How she wished it could be a two-way joining. But save when they were together in the flesh, they could merely speak back and forth, via a bone-conduction unit. Nevertheless, they were oath-sisters in truth. They were!)

"It's not telepathy," she said. "The channel won't carry but a tiny fraction of the total information. Most of what I experience is actually my own intuition, filling in the gaps. I've spent my career training that intuition. I'm trying to discover how accurate it really is."

"I understand," Flandry replied. "And you aren't linked continuously, or even as much as half the day, as a rule, let alone your absences from the planet. Still, you've been very deeply involved with this being. Your chief purpose has been to learn how to feel and think like her, hasn't it? Without that, there can be no true comprehension. So of course you've been affected yourself, in the most profound way."

They sat down on the rubbery deck and leaned against the bulkhead, side by side. "And therefore I won't know you, Banner, before I know more about Yewwl," he said. "Will you tell me?"

"How?" she sighed. "There's too much. Where can I begin?"

"Wherever you like. I do have a fair stock of so-called objective facts to go on by now, remember. You've taken me well into the biology—"

Although the Ramnuan atmosphere resembles Terra's percentagewise, the proportions of the minor constituents vary. Notably, we find less water vapor most places, because of the pressure and temperatures; more nitrogen oxides, because of frequent and tremendous lightning flashes; more carbon dioxide, hydrogen sulfide, and sulfur oxides, because of vulcanism. These would not be what killed us, if we breathed the air directly; they would simply make it acrid and malodorous. What we would die of, pretty soon, would be oxygen and nitrogen. They are not present at concentrations which are intolerable for a limited span, but their pressure, under seven gravities, would force them into our lungs and bloodstreams faster than we can stand. Incidentally, that pull by itself forbids us to leave our home-conditioned base for any long while. Our cardiovascular system isn't built for it. Gravanol and tight skinsuits help, but the stress quickly becomes too much.

Just the same, Ramnuan life reminds us of our kind in many ways. It employs proteins in water solution, carbohydrates, lipids, and the rest. The chemical details vary enormously. For example, the amino acids are not all identical; since weather provides abundant nitrates, nitrogen-fixing micro-organisms, while they do exist, are—like Terra's anaerobic bacteria—archaic forms of rather minor ecological significance; et cetera endlessly. In a broad sense, though, evolution has followed a similar course to ours. Here too it has founded a plant and an animal kingdom.

The critical secondary element is sulfur. It is so common in the environment, thanks to vulcanism, that biology has adopted it somewhat as Terran biology has adopted phosphorus. On Ramnu, sulfur is vital to several functions, including reproduction. It is usually taken up by plants as sulfate, or in the tissues which herbivores and carnivores eat. Where an area is deficient in it, life is sparse. Forest fires help, redistributing it in ash which the dense atmosphere disperses widely. Most important are certain microbes which can metabolize the pure element.

When it becomes freshly abundant, as around an active volcano, these organisms multiply until sheer numbers make them visible, a yellow smoke in air, a hue in water. Dying, they enrich the soil. This is the Golden Tide whose coming has brought fertility to land after land, whose dwindling has brought famine till populations died sufficiently back. The natives also transport sulfur, on a far smaller scale; their trade in it has conditioned their histories more than the salt trade has those of humans.

Given the oxygen concentration and the incidence of lightning, fires kindle easily and burn fiercely. Outside of wetlands, such a thing as a climax forest scarcely exists; woods burn down too often. Vegetation has made various adaptations to this, deep roots or bulbs, rapid reseeding, and the like. Most striking is that of the huge, diverse botanical family which we call pyrasphale. It synthesizes a silicon compound which makes it incombustible.

The pyrasphales have numerous analogies to the grasses of Terra or the yerbs of Hermes. They are comparative latecomers, that have taken over the larger part of most lands and proliferated into a bewildering variety of forms. Many do bear a superficial resemblance to this or that grass. Their appearance was doubtless responsible for a period of massive extinction about fifty million years ago; they crowded out older plants, and countless animals could not digest their fireproofing. Later herbivores have adjusted, either excreting it unchanged or breaking it down with the help of symbiotic microbes.

Pyrasphale has not displaced everything else. Where it reigns alone, that is apt to be by default. Ordinarily, a landscape covered by it has stands of trees, shrubs, thorn, or cane as well.

The animals of Ramnu exhibit their own abundant analogies to those of Terra, including two sexes, vertebrates and invertebrates, exothermic and endothermic metabolisms. The typical vertebrate has a head in front, with jaws, nose, two eyes, two ears; it bears four true limbs; commonly it sports a tail. But the differences exceed the likenesses.

Among the most obvious is the general smallness, under that gravity. Outside the seas, the very biggest creatures mass a couple of tonnes; and they inhabit regions of lake and swamp, where the water supports most of their weight as they browse around. A plain may teem with herds of assorted species, but nearly every one is dog-sized or less. An occasional horse-tall beast may loom majestic above them. It has a special feature, of which more later. Otherwise, at first it strikes a human odd to see a graviportal build on an animal no bigger than a collie. The gracile forms are tiny.

The long, cold nights set a premium on endothermy. Exotherms must find a place to sleep where they won't freeze (or, they hope, be dug up and eaten) or else start a new generation by sunset whose juvenile stage can survive. Plants have developed their own solutions to the same problem, including a family which secretes antifreeze and several families which make freezing a part of their life cycles.

An intermediate sort of animal has a high metabolism to keep warm at night but—outside the polar regions and highlands—must take shelter by day, lest it get too warm. Complete endothermy is harder to achieve than on Terra, since water evaporates reluctantly. The larger animals grow cooling surfaces such as big ears or dorsal fins.

Flyers face less difficulty in this regard, for their wings provide those surfaces; but it is worth noting that none have feathers. They are abundant on Ramnu, where the gravity is more or less offset by the thickness of the atmosphere. The swift drop of pressure with altitude does make most of them stay close to the ground. A few scavengers can soar high. Then there are the gliders; but of these, too, more later.

Among the land vertebrates, an order of viviparous endotherms exists which has no Terran paral- lel: the pleurochladoi. Between the fore- and hindlimbs, a pair of ribs has become the founda- tion, anchored to an elaborate scapular process, of two false limbs, which humans call extensors. It is thought that these lengths of muscle originated in a primitive, short-legged creature which thus found a way to hitch itself along a trifle faster. The develop- ment was so successful that descendants radiated into hundreds of kinds.

Extensors give added support; grasping, hauling, pushing, they give added locomotion. Hence they have enabled certain of their possessors to become as big as mustangs.

In quite a different direction, extensors produced the sub-order of gliding animals. These grew mem- branes from the forequarters to the tips of the ex- tensors, and from the tips to the hindquarters. The membranes doubtless began as a cooling device, which they remain, but they have elaborated into airfoils—vanes. Such a beast can fold them and run around freely. Or it can stiffen the extensors, thereby spreading the vanes, and glide down from a height. Given favorable currents, it can go astonish- ingly far in the dense air, or perform extraordinary maneuvers. Thereby it gets fruit, prey, escape from enemies, easy transportation.

Most gliders are bat-sized, but a few have become larger, and a few of these have become bipedal. Among them are the sophonts.

Red-gold, Niku waxed bright among the stars. In less than a day, it would be the sun.

Flandry saw how Banner's glance kept straying to its image in the screen. This was to have been a happy evenwatch, the last peaceful span they would know for a time they did not know—perhaps an eternity. Garbed in the finest they had along, they

sipped their drinks in between dances until Chives set forth the best dinner he was capable of. Afterward Flandry had him join them in a valedictory glass, but the batman said goodnight as soon as that was done. Now—

Cognac was mellow on the tongue, fragrant in the nostrils, ardent along the throat and in the blood. Flandry didn't smoke while he savored stuff as lordly as this. He did make it an obbligato to the sight and nearness of Banner. They were side by side; when she looked ahead, into the stars, he saw the proud profile. Tonight a silver circlet harnessed the tide of her mane. The hair flowed lustrous brown, touched by minute, endearing streaks of white. A bracelet Yewwl had given her, raw gemstones set in bronze, would have been barbarically massive on her left wrist, save that the casting was exquisite. She wore a deep-blue velvyl gown, long, low-cut, and though her bosom was small, the curve of it up toward her throat made him remember Botticelli.

He was not in love with her, nor—he supposed— she with him, except to the gentle degree that was only natural and that, in ordinary life, would only have added piquancy to friendship. He did find her attractive, and thought the cosmos of her as a person, in her own right, not merely because she was daughter to Max Abrams. So much had he come to respect her on this voyage that he no longer felt guilty about having brought her.

Soft in the background, music played as it had done for forty generations before theirs, the New World Symphony.

Abruptly she turned face and body about, toward him. The green eyes widened. "Dominic," she asked, "why are you here?"

"Huh?" he responded inelegantly. *Don't let her get too serious. Help her stay happy.* "Well, that depends on your exact meaning of the word 'why.' In an empirical sense, I am here because sixty-odd years ago, an operatic diva had an affair with a space captain. In the higher or philosophical sense—"

She interrupted by laying a hand over his. "Please don't clown. I want to understand." She sighed. "Though maybe you won't want to tell me. Then I won't insist; but I hope you will."

He surrendered. "What is it you'd like to know?"

"Why you are here—bound for Ramnu instead of Hermes." Quickly: "I know you had to investigate what Cairncross is hiding. If he really does plan a coup—"

Yes, I do believe that's his aim. What else? As Grand Duke, he's gone as far as he can, and he's known to be a man of vaulting ambition. He's popular among his people, and they are resentful of the Imperium; it'd be no trick to quietly collect personnel for the illicit preparation of war matériel, and he controls plenty of places where the work can go on in secret—Babur, Ramnu—When he's ready, when he announces his intention, men will flock to his standard. It won't take any enormous striking force if the operation is well organized. He can exploit surprise, punch through, kill Gerhart, and proclaim himself Emperor. When Terra lies hostage to his missiles, he won't be directly attacked.

Fighting will occur elsewhere, no doubt, but it will be between those who'll want to accept him and those who'll not. Many will. Gerhart is not beloved. Cairncross can set forth the claim that he is righting grievous wrongs and intends to right others; that in this dangerous era, the Empire needs the leader of greatest, proven ability; even that he has a dash of Argolid in his ancestry. A lot of Navy officers will feel they should go along with him simply to end the strife before it ruins too much, and because he is now the alternative to a throne back up for grabs. Others, as

*his cause gathers momentum, will deem it prudent
to join. Yes, Edwin has a good chance of pulling it off,
amply good for a warrior born.*

"—though things you've said about the Emperor
do make me wonder if you care what happens to
him," Banner stumbled onward.

Flandry scowled. "I don't, *per se*. However, he
isn't intolerably bad; in fact, he shows reasonable
intelligence and restraint. Besides, well, he is a son
of Hans, and I rather liked that old bastard. But
mainly, we can't afford a new civil war, and anybody
who'd start one is a monster."

Her fingers tightened across his. "You talked
about buying years for people to live in."

He nodded. "I'm no sentimentalist, but I've wit-
nessed wars. I don't relish the idea of sentient beings with their skins burnt off and their eyeballs
melted, but not yet able to die." He stopped. "Sorry.
That's not nice dinner table conversation."

She gave him a faint smile. "No, but I'm not a
perfectly nice person myself. All right, agreed, this
has to be prevented. Before it's too late, you have to
find out if a coup is in the works, and in that case get
proof that'll make the Navy act. You think probably
there's evidence in the Nikuan System. But why are
you going to collect it yourself? Wouldn't it be wiser
to proceed to Hermes and potter around, being
harmless? Meanwhile I could accompany men of
yours to Ramnu and they'd do the job."

Flandry shook his head. "I considered that, obviously," he replied; "but I've told you before, I'm
afraid Cairncross is almost ready to strike. I dare not
be leisurely."

"Still, you could have covered your ass, couldn't
you?"

He blinked, then laughed. "Perhaps. Though on
Hermes I'd be at Cairncross' mercy, you realize."

"But you could have made an excuse to stay

home, and dispatched a crew in secret," she persisted. "Feigned illness or whatnot. You're too clever for anybody to make you go where you don't want to."

"You're trying to flatter me," he said. "You're succeeding. As a matter of fact, with my usual humility I admit that you've pointed to the real reason. I've trained several excellent people, but none are quite as clever as me. None would have quite the probability of success that I do." He preened his mustache. "Also, to be honest, I confess I was getting bored. I was much overdue for raising a bit of hell."

Still her eyes would not release him. "Is that the whole truth, Dominic?"

He shrugged. "In a well-known phrase from an earlier empire, what is truth?"

Her tone shivered. "I think your underlying reason is this. The mission is dangerous. Failure means a terrible punishment for whoever went and got caught afterward. The fact that he went under your orders wouldn't save him from the wrath of a Grand Duke whose 'insulted honor' the Imperium would find it politic to avenge." She drew breath. "Dominic, you served under my father, and he was an officer of the old school. An officer does not send men to do anything he would not do himself. Isn't that it, dear?"

"Oh, I suppose a bit of it is," he grumbled.

Her glance dropped. How long the lashes lay, above those finely carven cheekbones. He saw the blood rise in face and bosom. "I felt sure, but I wanted to hear it from you," she whispered. "We've got plenty of noble titles around these days, but damn few noble spirits."

"Oh, hai, hai," he protested. "You know better. I lie, I steal, I cheat, I kill, I fornicate and commit adultery, I use shocking language, I covet, and once I had occasion to make a graven image. Now can we relax and enjoy our evening?''

She raised her countenance to his. Her smile brightened. "Oh, yes," she said. "Why, in your company I'd expect to enjoy exile."

They had talked about that, what to do if the mission failed but they survived. A court martial would find him guilty of worse than insubordination; defiance of a direct Imperial command was treason. She was an accomplice. The maximum penalty was death, but Flandry feared they would get the "lighter" sentence of life enslavement. He didn't propose to risk that. He'd steer for a remote planet where he could assume a new identity, unless he decided to seek asylum in the Domain of Ythri or collect a shipful of kindred souls and fare off into the altogether unknown.

Banner had agreed, in pain. She had far more to lose than he did, a mother, a brother and sister and their families, Yewwl and her lifework.

Has she found hope, now, beyond the wreckage of hope? His heart sprang for joy.

She leaned close. Her blush had faded to a glow, her look and voice were steady. "Dominic, dear," she said, "ever since that hour in the gym, you've been the perfect knight. It isn't necessary any longer."

VII

Ramnu swelled steadily in the forward screen, until it owned the sky and its dayside radiance drowned stars out of vision. The colors were mostly white upon azure, like Terra's, though a golden tinge lay across them in this weaker, mellower sunlight. Cloud patterns were not the same, but wider spread and more in the form of bands, spots, and sheets than of swirls; surface features were hidden from space, save as vague shadowiness here and there. The night side glimmered ghostly under moonlight and starlight. Brief, tiny fire-streaks near the terminator betokened monstrous lightning strokes. Brought into being by a magnetic field less than Jovian but stronger than Terran, auroras shook their flags for an incoming man to see above polar darkness.

Flandry sat at the pilot console. *Hooligan* continued doing the basic navigation and steering herself, but he wanted his hand and judgment upon her, that he might arrive in secret. Besides, he meant to use the instruments in the control section to study the moons and any possible traffic in the system.

He passed close enough by Diris, the innermost, that he could make out Port Lulang, the scientific base. It was a huddle of domes, hemicylinders, masts, dishes, beside a spacefield, in the middle of a large, symmetrical formation oddly like Sullivan's Hoofprint on Io; little that was Cynthian remained except the name. Otherwise the satellite was nearly featureless. Once it had exceeded his mother world in size; but the supernova whiffed away everything above its metallic core. Probably naught whatsoever would have survived, had not the shrunken bulk of

Ramnu given some shielding. As the melted ball cooled to solidity, no asteroids or meteoroids smote to crater it. Those had been turned into gas, and dissipated with the rest of the nebula among the stars.

Tiglaia showed a measure of ruggedness; it had kept the mass to generate orogenic forces. Elaveli, outermost and largest, bore mountains, sharp-

edged as when first they were uplifted.

Flandry probed toward the latter, but got no sight of Port Asmundsen, the industrial base there. He wasn't observing from the proper angle, and dared not accelerate into a different course lest he be noticed. If his idea about Cairncross was right, these days the expanded facilities included war-craft. Anyway, Banner had confirmed that nothing unusual was apparent from outside. Whatever evil was hatching did so under camouflage or in manmade caverns. Neutrino detectors spoke of substantial nuclear powerplants. *Yes, they impress me as being rather more than required by mining operations. Having an exposed planetary core makes the enterprise worthwhile for Hermes —but scarcely this profitable, when the same metals are available closer to home.*

As for Dukeston — His look strayed back to Ramnu. The commercial base on the planet had likewise been a minor thing, until lately. A sulfur-rich marshland produced certain biologicals, notably a fine-grained hardwood and the antibiotic oricin, effective against the Hermetian disease cuprodermy. They were barely cheaper to obtain here and to ship back than to synthesize. They might not have been were not the nearby Chromatic Hills a well-endowed source of palladium and other minerals.

Why had Dukeston, too, seen considerable recent growth? And why had it, too, become hard to enter and to deal with? True, it and Wainwright Station were separated by five thousand kilometers of continent. A parameter in choosing the site for it had been the desire that its cultural influence reach only the natives in its vicinity, not those whom the xenologists made their principal subjects of study. Nevertheless, people used to flit freely back and forth, often just to visit. General Enterprises used to be generous in supplying the Ramnu Research Foundation with help, equipment, materials.

But under the present director, Nigel Broderick—Well, he explained the niggardliness and the infrequency of contact by declaring that the expansion itself, under adverse conditions, took virtually all the resources at his beck. The undertaking was a part of great Duke Edwin's far-sighted plan for restoring the glory and prosperity of Hermes. His

Grace had ordered stringent security measures against the possibility of sabotage, in these uneasy times. No exceptions could be made, since a naive scientist might innocently pass information to the wrong persons. If this attitude seemed exaggerated, that was because you did not know the ramifications of the whole situation. His Grace alone did that, and ours was not to question him.

Which I aim to do, if time and chance allow, Flandry thought. *Oh, I am a bad, rebellious boy, I am. I actually nourish a few doubts about the wisdom and benevolence of statesmen.*

Hooligan set down with admirable smoothness, considering. For a few minutes Flandry was addressing the hastily summoned ground control officer. (He was a young fellow named Ivan Polevoy, whose primary job was electronician.) The station spacecraft occupied the sole proper connection to the interior which the minuscule field possessed. It would be necessary to send a car for the newcomers.

Having spoken his thanks and requested that no word of this go out —"Dr. Abrams will tell you why, in due course"—Flandry made his routine check of guardian devices: irrespective of the fact that Chives would stay aboard till it was certain that no backup would be needed. Meanwhile his glance roved around outside. Port Wainwright consisted of several conjoined buildings, whose low profiles and deep foundations were designed for this world. A pole displayed a flag of gaudy, fluorescent stripes. Beyond, the landscape reached tremendous.

Niku stood at early afternoon, ruddy-aureate in an opalescent heaven; its light suffused the hazy air in a way to remind of autumn on Terra. Nothing else was like home. Broad, gray-green, a river flowed past more swiftly than it should, casting spray that lingered shining above rocks and current-whirls. The woods on the opposite shore were not dense, though they stretched out of sight. Squat brown boles sprouted withy-like branches with outsize leaves of cupped form and hues of dark olive, amber, or russet. A slow, heavy breeze sent the stalks rippling about and stirred the underbrush.

On this bank and eastward was open country, a plain dominated by pyrasphale. Most of that resembled tall grass wherein the wind roused waves. Its dull tawniness was relieved in place by stands of trees or canes, by white plumes and vivid blossoms. He couldn't see through mistiness to the remote horizon, but he made out a kopje in that direction; and northward, a darkening must be mountains, for a volcano sent smoke aloft from there. The pillar of black widened quickly, to form a mushroom shape whose top drifted away like fog.

Leathery wings cruised low overhead, big in proportion to the bodies they upheld. He knew that herds of animals were out in the pyrasphale, but it hid their low shapes from him. A family of giants loomed above, not far off, grazing with the calm of creatures which had no natural enemies. Humans refrained from hunting near the station, and no native Ramnuans were around at the moment.

He watched the beasts interestedly, for he recognized them as wild onsars. Domesticated, the onsar was the foundation of sophont life over much of the world. It was more than a carrier of riders and burdens; it was a platform from which a hunter could see quarry afar, and then launch himself on a long glide. Before they had that help, the Ramnuans were mostly confined to the forests and the hilliest parts of this planet, whose land surface consisted largely of savannah, pampa, prairie, veldt, and steppe.

An onsar stood big enough for a man to mount, if

he wouldn't mind his feet dangling close to the ground. Its build was vaguely suggestive of a rhinoceros, given a high hump at the forequarters and a high black triangle of dorsal fin on the after half of the back. The skin was gray, sparsely brown-haired save on the big-eared, curve-muzzled head, where it grew thicker. Most conspicuous to Flandry were the extensors. They seemed akin to a pair of elephants' trunks, sprouting from muscular masses behind the hump, but they terminated in pads and clawed, prehensile tendrils.

"Excuse me, sir," Chives reminded from the entrance.

Flandry realized that a sealed car was on its way toward *Hooligan*. Shaking himself, he hurried to join Banner. She waited at the main personnel airlock. "Welcome home," he said.

"Welcome to my home, Dominic," she answered softly. They exchanged a kiss.

The car halted alongside and extended a gang tube from its metal shell. When that had snugly fitted itself around the lock, Banner valved through. Flandry followed. He had done this kind of thing before, but each planet was a special case requiring special configurations of equipment, and he was glad to let her coach him. Safety harness—careful positioning on the conveyor belt—when inside the chassis, doubly careful crawling into a seat, and grateful relaxation as it reclined—The vehicle had no grav generators, and for this short a trip it carried no drugs or body supports. Seven-plus times his normal weight dragged at Flandry like a troll. Breath strained, heart slugged, every movement was leaden, he felt his cheeks sag downward and avoided looking at the woman; consciousness began to blur at the edges.

The robopilot disengaged, retracted the tube, drove rapidly over the ferrocrete. It cycled through

into the garage pretty fast, too, and blessed light-
ness returned.

Banner scrambled forth. A gaunt, middle-aged
man stood waiting. "How did your mission go?" he
asked immediately, anxiously. Long-term personnel here were devoted folk.

"That's quite a story," she told him in a clipped
voice. "Admiral Sir Dominic Flandry, I'd like you to
meet Huang Shao-Yi, our deputy director and one
blaze of a good linguist."

"An honor, sir."—"The honor is mine, Dr.
Huang."

"What's been happening?" burst from Banner.

Huang shrugged. "Little out of the ordinary.
Yewwl allowed us at last to bring her back. I believe
she's presently in the Lake Roah neighborhood, and
is recovering well from her loss."

Banner nodded. "She would. She doesn't surrender. I want to get in touch at once."

"But—" Huang said at her retreating form. "But
you've just arrived, you must be tired, we want to
receive you properly, and our distinguished
guest—"

"Your distinguished guest is in an ant-bitten
hurry himself," Flandry said, and followed Banner.
Huang stayed behind. He had learned the ways of
his chief.

Striding through rooms and passages, Flandry
saw how the station had gone shabby-comfortable
during centuries of use. Murals by amateurs
brightened walls; planters held beds of flowers and
fresh vegetables; playback simulated windows
opening on a dozen distant worlds. The hour
chanced to be late on human clocks, and most
people were in the recreation facilities or their private apartments. What few were not and encountered Banner greeted her with pleasure. She might
be on the austere and reticent side, Flandry

thought, but she was well-liked, and that was well-deserved.

She entered her centrum. He saw how she trembled as she sat down amidst the instruments which bristled about her chair. He stroked her head. She gave him an absent-minded smile and set about lowering the helmet. He stepped back.

She grew busy making adjustments. Meters flickered, telltales blinked in the dimness of the chamber. It was quiet here; only a murmur of the thick breeze outside penetrated. At present, in its variant pattern, station air was cool, moist, bearing a smell of Terran seas.

The screen before Banner flickered to life. Flandry could see it over her shoulder if he leaned down and forward. She laid her palms on two plates in the arms of her chair. What sensations came to her from them, she would interpret as perceptions of the world beyond these walls. She had told him that by now they seemed almost like the real thing.

"Yewwl," she called low, and added words in a purring, ofttimes mewing or snarling language unknown to him. A vocalizer circuit transformed them into sounds that were clear to a Ramnuan, whose mouth and throat were not made like hers. "Ee-yah, Yewwl."

Flandry must content himself with what was in the screen. That was remarkably clear, given the handicaps under which the system labored. Colors, perspectives, contours did appear subtly strange, until he remembered that the apparatus tried to duplicate what alien eyes saw, as they did.

A hand lifted into sight—Yewwl's, perhaps raised in surprise when the message came. It was probably the most humanoid thing about her, the thumb and four fingers laid out very similarly to his. They were short, though, their nails were sharp and yellow, the entire hand was densely muscular, and tan fur covered it.

She was indoors, doubtless in a ranch house belonging to a family of her clan. Furnishing was simple but handsome. On a couch in view sat a pair of natives who must be kinfolk, male and female. No matter how many pictures he had studied while traveling, Flandry focused his whole attention on them.

They were both bipeds who would stand slightly over a meter. Extreme stockiness might have seemed grotesque, were it not clear that their build was what enabled them to move gracefully. The feet were four-toed, clawed, big even in proportion. The lower torso was nearly rigid for support, the high pelvic girdle making it impossible to bend over—not a good idea on Ramnu anyhow—and requiring them to squat instead. This also forced the young to be born tiny, after a short gestation; male and female both had pouches on the belly to protect an infant till it had developed further. These and the genitalia did not come to Flandry's vision, for the beings happened to be dressed: in garments vaguely resembling hospital gowns, decking the front, the most convenient if you had vanes in back. Fur grew everywhere, save for footsoles and the insides of the hands.

The head was round. Its face could be called either blunt-muzzled or platyrrhine and prognathous; the jaw was heavy and had a chin, the brow swelled lofty. The mouth was wide, thin-lipped for the sucking of blood and juices and for the feeding of infants; yellow fangs bespoke a carnivore, though not an obligate one. The ears sat far up, pointed and mobile. The eyes were beautiful—big, golden, variable of pupils, adaptable to night. The whole countenance made Flandry recall, the least bit, a Terran lynx.

From the back, under the shoulders, sprang the

extensors. The female had brought hers around in front, making a sort of cloak; perhaps she was cold, in this gathering ice age. The male had spread his when reacting to Banner, as if readying for a glide. From behind his neck, the membranes of the vanes stretched thinly furred, nearly a meter on either side, to the ends of the extensors: thence downward, semicircularly, to the buttocks. Flandry knew they were attached along the entire back, above the spine. They were no simple flaps of skin, they were muscular tissue, heavily vascularized, their nerve endings providing a great deal of sensory input, their complex ripplings and attitudes providing a body language that humans would never really be able to interpret.

As Flandry watched, the male relaxed, lowered his extensors till the vanes hung in folds behind him, and settled himself alertly. Belike Yewwl had told her companions what was occurring.

Flandry stole a look at Banner's face. It was intent with the desperation of this hour, but it was likewise rapt; she had gone beyond him. She barely whispered what she said. When she stopped to listen, she alone heard.

The view in the screen shifted jerkily, then changed, changed, changed. Yewwl had jumped to her feet, was pacing—might be cursing or yelling, for all he could tell. The message she got had carried a shock.

Flandry and Banner had planned it together, but today he must merely guess how matters went. What she was asking was fearsome.

In the end, when she had blanked the screen and disconnected herself, she slumped, eyes closed, breathing hard, shivering. Sweat stood forth on a pale visage.

Flandry cupped her cheeks between his hands. "How are you?" he asked, half afraid.

The green gaze opened as she tilted her head back. "Oh, *I'm* all right," she said faintly.

"She—will she—"

The woman nodded. "Yes. She doesn't understand much of what it's about. How could she? But if nothing else, out of loyalty, she'll believe her oath-sister, that this has to be done before her country can be saved." A sigh. "May that be true."

He would have tried to comfort her, but time lashed him. "Shall we have her flitted to Mount Gungnor?"

"No." Banner's self-possession returned fast. She straightened; her tone briskened. "No point in that. In fact, it'd be counterproductive. Best she proceed overland, sending messengers out on either side to ask other leaders if they'll meet her along the way. She has to persuade them to go along with the idea, you see, and with her in person. Else she'd be a single individual arriving at the Volcano, who could speak for her immediate family at best. Whereas, leading a delegation from what amounts to the whole of Kulembarach, and maybe a couple of neighbors clans as well—do you see?"

Flandry frowned. "How long will this take?"

"M-m. . . . Three or four Terran days, I'd guess. She's fairly close to the mountain, and Ramnuans can travel fast when they want to."

Flandry clicked his tongue. "You're cutting it molecular fine. The Duke can't be much further behind us than that. Allowing a short while for him to decide on Hermes what to do, and getting an expedition here from there—"

"It can't be helped, dear." Banner rose. "I'll monitor Yewwl closely, of course, and urge her to keep moving. Furthermore, you know some of my younger colleagues have links like mine, to different individuals, through a wide territory. None are anything like as close as this relationship; but we can make contact, we can request them to pass the word on and to rendezvous with Yewwl if possible. We can scarcely explain why, either to those colleagues or their subjects. But I think several will oblige, out of curiosity and friendship. That should help."

"Well, you're the expert," he said reluctantly. "As for myself meanwhile, I'm a master of the science and art of heelcooling."

She chuckled. "You'll be busy aplenty if I know you, studying maps and data banks, talking to people, laying contingency plans. And . . . we do want some time in between for ourselves, don't we?"

He laughed and caught her to him. Last night-watch had not been spectacular, but in its manyfold ways it had been good, as liking deepened with intimacy. He was a little old for the spectacular, anyway.

VIII

Yewwl fared north from the house by Lake Roah in company, as befitted a ranking matron of the clan on her way to meet with her peers on the Volcano. She and certain of her retainers had been visiting her oldest son—he and his sister her last surviving children—and his family; they had discussed combining their ranches, now that her husband and youngsters were gone. He rode off at her side, followed by half a dozen of his own hands. His wife would manage the place in his absence . . . perhaps better than in his presence, Yewwl thought tartly, for Skogda was an over-impulsive sort.

Before leaving, they dispatched couriers to homesteads that were not too far off. These went afoot, or a-glide when possible, faster than onsars. Yewwl's party was mounted, since there was no point in arriving ahead of a quorum. Besides, it suited her dignity and ⸺ she would need that at her goal, antagonistic to her as many of the Seekers were. Her route she laid out to pass by some more households, where she requested the heads to come along. All did. These stops were brief, and otherwise they made none, so progress was rapid. Eventually folk and onsars would have to sleep, but they could keep moving without rest for most of a day or night, and often did.

Thus Yewwl came to the Volcano, in the ancient manner of her people. The Kulembarach *dzai'h'ü*—"clan," humans called it, for lack of a better word that they could pronounce—was showing by the number of its representatives present that most of it

would support her, once news of her intent had spread throughout the territory. That was to be expected. Not only were its members her kin, in various degrees; she took a foremost role, her opinions carried weight, in the yearly moot, when leaders of households gathered to discuss matters of mutual concern (and to trade, gossip, arrange marriages and private ventures, play games, revel, make Oneness). Moreover, two from different territories, Arachan and Raava, had joined the group.

This was important. The Lord of the Volcano could not act on behalf of the clans together, when just a single one had speakers present. But if Zh of Arachan and Ngaru of Raava raised no objection, he could, if he saw fit, accede to the wish of Kulembarach—in a matter like this, which presumably would involve no major commitment of everybody else.

Hard though the band traveled, day was drawing to an end when they reached the mountain. From the trail which wound up its flank, Yewwl saw far across the plain beneath, aglow in long red sunrays. Clouds, banked murky toward the northeast, told of a storm that would arrive with the early dusk . . . but by then, she remembered, or soon after, she would be on the distant side of it, in lands where full night would have fallen . . . if she could carry out this first part of Banner's enigmatic plan. . . .

'Cold streamed downward from the snows which covered the upper half of Mount Gungnor, and which yearly lay thicker. Moltenness laired underneath; steam from fumaroles blew startlingly white against yellow evening overcast and black smoke from the crater. A stream flowed out of a place where melt water had formed a spring. It cascaded down the slopes in noise and spray. The Golden Tide colored it, and drifted in streamers on muttering breezes. Yewwl could smell and taste the pungency of the life-bestower on every breath; what weariness was in her dropped away.

Because of that potent substance, the lower sides of the mountain were not bare. Their darkness was crusted with color, tiny plants that etched a root-hold for themselves in the rock, and above them buzzed equally minute flying things, whose wings glittered. Yet those had become few, and Yewwl saw more brown patches, frost-killed, across the reaches than there had been when last she was here. Rounding a shoulder that had barred her view northward, she saw the Guardian range rearing over the horizon, and it shimmered blue with the Ice.

The same curve in the trail brought her out onto a plateau which jutted ledge-like from the steeps. This was her goal. A turf of low nullfire, lately gone sere, decked the top of it; hoofbeats, which had rung on the way up, now padded. Boldly near the prec-ipice edge reared the hall that the clans had raised for the Lords of the Volcano to inhabit, in that won-derful age when the land suddenly redoubled its fertility and folk grew in number until they needed more than their kin-moots to maintain law. The building was of stone, long and broad, shale-roofed. Flanking the main door were six weather-worn statues, the Forebears of each clan. A seventh, spear in hand, faced outward at the end of the rows. It stood for the chosen family, bred out of all the clans, from which the successive Lords were elected. It stood armed, peering over the cliff, as though to keep ward against those little-known people, beyond the territories, whose ways were not the ways of the clans.

The Lord and his household lived by hunting, not ranching: for the country around the foot of the mountain was of course incredibly rich, or had been. However, just as had happened elsewhere, a small settlement of sedentary artisans had grown up. From one of the half-timbered cottages clustered nearby, Yewwl heard the clamor of iron being forged; from another came the hum of a loom-wheel; from a third drifted the acrid odors of tanning leather. These died out as persons grew aware of visitors and emerged to see.

Erelong someone also left a building which stood by itself at the far end of the plateau. It was oldest by centuries, much like the hall but the stone of it made smooth-edged, the carvings blurred, by untold rains, gritty winds, acid fumes — even in this thin air. Changeless, a great, faceted crystal caught the light where it was inset above the entrance. It proclaimed this a sanctuary of the College. Here, as in houses they owned elsewhere, the Seekers of Wisdom kept books, instruments, ceremonial gear, mysteries.

At first, those who stepped out, male and female, were those who lived there, together with their children. They numbered ten adults. Half were young, initiates studying for higher orders, meanwhile acting as caretakers, copyists, handlers of routine College business. The rest were aging; they lacked the gifts needed to attain an upper degree, and were resigned to that. Yewwl had no quarrel with any of these; in truth, she seldom encountered them.

But then a different figure trod from inside, male, clad throat to feet in a white apron, bearing a gilt harp under his left arm and a bronze chaplet on his brows. Across a kilometer, Yewwl knew him. Her vanes snapped wide. She bristled. A hiss went between her fangs.

Skogda brushed a vane of his across hers. The play beneath the skin said: *I am with you, Mother, whatever may happen. What alarms you?*

"Erannda," she told him, and pointed her ears at the senior Seeker. "Ill luck that he's not exacting

hospitality from a homestead afar." She willed the tension out of her muscles. "I'll not let him check me. He'll try, but he can't sing away the truth."

Inwardly, she wondered: *Truth? I dare not speak truth myself, what little of it I grasp. To hear the real purpose of my mission would bewilder them utterly. The Lord would refuse to act, in a matter so weird and dangerous, without first holding a full assembly of clan-heads; and most of my own following would agree he was right.*

By law and custom he would be, too. (Maybe the most baffling and disturbing thing about the star-folk is the way they submit their wills, their fates, to the will of others, whom they may never even have met. That is, if I have discerned what Banner has tried over the years to explain to me. Sometimes I have hoped I am mistaken about this.)

But by the time a full assembly can be gathered, it would be too late. Banner said we likeliest have less than a day to do what must be done . . . whatever that is, beyond my part in it. Else a wrong will happen, and the star-folk will not be able to drive the Ice back.

I do not understand, really. I can only keep faith with my oath-sister, who has asked for my help.

But Banner, will you help me in turn? I'll need you to strengthen my wits against Erannda's. Banner, send your voice back into my head. Soon. Please.

Meanwhile, she would not quail. "Come!" she cried, and her body added: *Come in style!* She straightened to present her jeweled leather breastplate. She displayed her vanes at full. She drew her knife and held the blade on high. Her foot-claws pricked the extensors of her onsar, and the gait of the beast became a rapid swing. Behind her, drawing haughtiness from her, thundered two score of householders and retainers.

The cottage dwellers stood humbly aside. Useful though they were, their sort could not claim the respect due a hunter, herder, or Seeker; for they did not kill their own food, nor did they range freely about.

Yewwl's band drew rein outside the hall. Skogda winded the horn that announced their coming. Echoes flew shrill through the evening. It would have been improper for the Lord of the Volcano to come forth, as if out of curiosity, before he got such a call. Now he did. A scarlet cloth, wrapped around brow and neck, streamed down his front to the ground. He carried a spear, which he gravely dipped and left thrust in the turf, a sign of welcome.

His family and servants were at his back, less impressive. They were not numerous, either, for none but he, his wife, and their offspring dwelt here, together with servants. The rest of his kin were below the mountain, save for those who had chosen to join the College or to be adopted into a clan. They were the people from whom an assembly would choose his successor, after his death.

Yewwl thought the last election could well have gone differently. Wion was not the keenest-minded person alive. He did get good advice from his wife, better than from the College which was supposed to supply him with councillors. She was a female of Arrohdzaroch. But she could not sit beside him at the meeting. The ancestors had decided that the Lord of the Volcano must always be male, to counterbalance the preponderance of females who took the initiative in household and clan affairs.

Erannda was approaching. Yewwl dismounted. "May you ever be swift in the chase," she greeted Wion formally. "We are come on behalf of many more, to lay for them and ourselves a demand upon your stewardship."

Oil lamps brightened the meeting room in the hall, bringing frescos to vivid life. An iron stove at

either end held outside chill at bay. Lamps, stoves, maps, medicines, windmills, printing, water-powered machinery . . . above all, knowledge of this world and its universe, and an eagerness to learn more . . . how much had the star-folk given!

Else the chamber was not changed from of old, nor were the procedures. Wion sat on a dais between carven beasts, confronting two rows of tiered benches for the visitors. Whoever would speak raised an arm, was recognized by the Lord of the Volcano, and stepped or glided down to stand before him. This being much less than a full assembly, everyone was close in and matters went faster than usual.

Yewwl addressed them: "I need not relate how cold, hunger, and suffering range across our country in advance of the Ice, and how these can but worsen, and most of us die, as it moves onward. We have talked of what we might do. Some would flee south, some would stay and become hunters entirely, some have still other ideas in pouch. But any such action will cost us heavily at best. Have we no better hope?

"You know what the star-folk have taught us. You know they have always held, in the House of the Banner, that they will not give us what we cannot learn to make for ourselves, lest we become dependent on it and then one day they must leave us. What we have gotten from them has led us to progress of our own, slower than we might like but firmly rooted and ever growing. Think of better steel than aforetime, or glassmaking, or painkillers and deep surgery, or postal couriers, or what else you will. Yet it is no longer enough, when the Ice is coming. Unaided, we will lose it all; our descendants will forget.

"You know, too, that I am intimate with the chieftain of the star-folk, Banner herself." *Oath-sister*,

where are you? You promised you would join me.
"You know I have asked her for their help, and she
has told me this lies not within her power. But she
has told me further, of late, that perhaps help may
be gotten elsewhere."

Wion stiffened on his seat. The Seekers present
remained impassive as was their wont, save for
Erannda, who half spread his vanes and crooked his
fingers as if to attack.

"You wonder how this may be," Yewwl continued.
"It—" She broke off. The voice was in her.

—"Yewwl, are you awake? Do you want me? Good.
. . . Oh, has your meeting begun already? I'm sorry.
I didn't think you'd arrive so fast, and—" a hesita-
tion; a shyness?—"private matters engaged me
more than they should have. How are you faring?
What can I do?"

Wion leaned forward. "Is aught amiss, clan-
head?" he asked. Eyes stared from the benches.

"No. I, I pause to gather words," Yewwl said. "I
wish to put things as briefly as may be, lest we
wrangle till nightfall."

—"Don't you want them to know I'm listening?"
Banner asked.

—"No, best not, I believe," Yewwl replied in her
hidden speech. "Erannda is here, by vile luck.
You've seen how he hates your kind. Give him no
arrows for his quiver."

There flashed through her: *Once the Seekers of
Wisdom alone possessed the high knowledge, arcane
mysteries, healing, poetry, music, history. Traveling
from stead to stead, they were the carriers of news
and of lore about distant places. They counselled,
mediated, consoled, heartened, chastised, taught,
set a lofty example. Yes, our ancestors did right to
hold them in awe.*

*That is gone. Respect remains, unless among the
most impatient of the young. The Seekers still do*

good. They could do more. But for that, they must change, as the rest of us have changed, because of the star-folk. Some of the Seekers are willing. Others are not. Erannda leads that faction; and many in the clans still heed him.

She hastened to inform Banner of what had happened thus far: fortunately, very little. The unseen presence fell silent, and Yewwl resumed speaking:

"You may or may not be aware that the star-folk maintain a second outpost." *And outposts on two moons, but best not remind them of that. Erannda calls it a defilement.* "It is no secret; sometimes people have come here from there. However, yon settlement has had nothing to do with us, since it lies far off, beyond the territories and what we know of the wilderness. Thus we have had no cause to think about it.

"I have newly learned that it is not like the House of the Banner. It is larger, stronger, and its purpose is not simply to gather knowledge, but to maintain industries. Furthermore, its chiefs have more freedom of decision. As near as I have learned"—*which is not near at all, for I cannot understand; but my oath-sister would not lie to me*—"they can act even in weighty matters, without having first to get permission elsewhere.

"I, my following, and those for whom we speak propose this. Let me take a party there and ask for help. I cannot foresay if they will grant it; and if they will, I cannot foresay what form it may take. Perhaps they will give us firearms, that we may hunt more easily; perhaps they will let us have onsarless vehicles; perhaps they will supply us with fireless heat-makers; perhaps they will build huge, warm shelters for our herds—I know not, and I have not ventured to ask Banner."

No need. She has long since told me that such things are possible, yes, that it is possible to turn the

Ice back, but she and her fellows do not command the means, nor has she been able to get the yea of those who do.

"For this, we would no doubt have to make return. What, I do not know either. Trade, maybe; we have furs, hides, minerals. Labor, maybe; they might need native hands. The cost may prove too much and the clans refuse to pay. Very well, then. But it may not. The bargain may actually leave us better off than we ever were before.

"I propose to go ask, and negotiate if I can, and bring back word for an assembly to consider. To do this, I must go for our whole folk.

"Therefore, Lord of the Volcano, I, my following, and those for whom we speak demand of you that you grant us the right to act on behalf of the clans, and give me a letter attesting that this is so."

Yewwl snapped her vanes open and shut, to show that she had finished, and waited for questions.

They seethed about her. Was it not a dangerous journey, and many days in length? "Yes, but I am willing, and have friends who are willing too. How else can I strike back at the Ice, that robbed me of my darlings?"

Why could the party not simply be flown there? "We cannot breathe air as thin as the star-folk do. Not for years has the House of the Banner possessed a large flying machine with a cabin that can be left open, since it was wrecked in a dusk-storm. They have lacked the wealth to replace it. Their lesser vehicles can carry but a single person besides the pilot, and he would fall ill of heaviness on so long a flight."

Why cannot Banner herself go speak for us, or talk across distance as we know they are able to? "She fears she would be refused. Remember, the rule that she is under forbids giving us things like that. She doubts if I am being wise. Also, her kind are not innocent of rivalries and jealousies. The other chiefs might not welcome a proposal that would put her in the lead, yet listen to us if she is out of it."

Several more; and then Erannda came down, and Yewwl whispered, unheard here—"Now the fight begins."

Tall in his white garb, the Seeker struck a shivery chord from his harp. Silence pounced and gripped. His bard's voice rolled forth:

"Lord of the Volcano, colleagues, clanfolk, hear me. Harken when I say that this is either the maddest thought that ever was flung out, or else the evillest.

"Slowly have the aliens wrought among us, oh, very slowly and cunningly. Centuries have passed since first they came, avowing they did but wish to learn of us and of our country. Be it confessed, the College of those days welcomed them, seeing in them kindred spirits, and hoping in turn to range through new realms of knowledge. Yes, we too trusted them . . . in those days. But the College has a long memory; and today we look back, against the wind of time, and what we see is not what we endure.

"Piece by piece, the new things, the new words slipped in among us; and we thought they were good, and never paused to reckon the cost. New skills, new arts and crafts seemed to make life richer; but it came to pass that those who practiced them could not be free rovers, nor could each household provide for every need of its own. So died the wholeness of the folk.

"Behold this chaplet. It has been given from old hand to young hand for five hundred years. It can never be replaced. The making of such beauty in bronze is lost to our craftspeople. This may seem little, when instead we have steel; but the ugly coppersmithing of today cannot uplift the soul, and this is but the smallest token of the emptiness within us. Who now sings the ancient epics, who now honors the ancient wisdom and righteousness? The links of kinship corrode, as youth mocks at age and wants its way in everything. And why not? Is not our whole world a mere dust-fleck adrift in limitless, meaningless hollowness? Are we ourselves anything save wind made flesh, chance-formed, impotent, and foredoomed? *This* is the teaching the strangers have sent seeping into us, a teaching of despair so deep that few of us even recognize it as despair."

The harp rang. "But you have heard me chant this lay before. What of the present gathering? What shall we say?

"I bid you think. Yewwl has never hidden that she is the creature of an alien. What she does keep hidden is what that alien may have bidden her do, for its cold purposes. Long have they declared, at the House of the Banner, that we must not become dependent for our lives on things of theirs. This is true; but has it been a truth uttered to lull our wariness? For at last Yewwl proposes that we do indeed make such things necessary to our survival. I tell you, if that happens, we will be helpless before the demands of their makers. And what might those demands be? Who can tell? Yewwl herself admits she does not understand the strangers.

"Perhaps"—sarcasm ran venomous—"she is honest in her intent, in what she thinks she has said. Perhaps. But then, how can she hope to deal for us? What miscomprehensions might result, and what disasters follow? Better the glacier grind down across this whole country, and we flee to impoverished exile. At least we will remain free.

"Deny yonder witch. Cast her hence!"

The harp snarled to a finish.

Skogda sprang onto his bench, vanes wide. "You slime-soul, you dare speak thus of my mother!" he yelled. Almost, he launched himself against the Seeker. Two friends barely pulled him down and quieted him.

Erannda gave Yewwl a triumphant look. "That," he murmured, "deserves I put a satire upon him, and upon you."

—"Banner, what shall I do? I haven't his word-skill. If he makes a poem against me, I will be unheeded in council for the rest of my world-faring."

—"Oh! . . . But hold, Yewwl, don't panic, stand fast. I thought about this, that you might someday run into just this danger, years ago. I didn't discuss it with you, because it was a nasty subject, for you much more than for me; but I did prepare—"

Wion stirred on the dais. "It is a terrible thing you would do, Erannda," he warned. "Worse than the outburst of a way-wearied young male calls for. Such excess could bring reproach on you and the whole College. Best let him humble himself to you."

"I will that," Erannda replied, "if his mother and her gang will abandon their crazy scheme."

Banner had been whispering, fast and fiercely. The sense of her nearness in spirit sufficed by itself to kindle the heart anew. Yewwl stood forth and said:

"No. Are we not yet gorged with senseless rantings? What does he preach but fear and subservience—fear of tomorrow, subservience first to him and later to doom? Yes, the star-folk have caused changes, and in those changes is loss. But would you call it wrong that as your child grows, you lose the warmth of his little body in your pouch? Do you not, instead, rejoice to watch him soar forth?

"What threat have the star-folk ever been, save to those who would fetter us down and require we honor them into the bargain? The threat is from *them*, I tell you. If they prevail, everything we have achieved will perish, and likewise countless of us and our children and children's children. Shall we not even have a chance to seek help?''

Her audience listened aghast. Nobody had ever defied a senior Seeker thus openly, and before the very Lord of the Volcano.

Yewwl's words had been her own, following the advice she received from Banner. Having uttered them, she stalked toward Erannda, her vanes open, fur a-bristle, fangs bare. She said, before she herself could be appalled at what it was:

''I will lay a satire on you instead, old one, that all may ken you for what you truly are.''

He controlled his rage, made his harp laugh, and retorted, ''You? And what poetics have you studied?''

''I begin,'' she answered, halting close to him. And she declaimed Banner's words, as they were given her:

''*Wind, be the witness of this withering!*
Carry abroad, crying, calling,
The name I shall name. Let nobody
Forget who the fool was, or fail
To know how never once the not-wise
Had counsel worth keeping, in time of care—''

''Stop!'' he yelled. As he lurched back, his harp dropped to the clay floor.

He would have needed a night or longer to compose his satire. She threw hers at him, in perfect form, on the instant.

—''Don't be vengeful,'' Banner urged. ''Leave him a way out.''

—''Oh, yes,'' Yewwl agreed. Pity surprised her.

Erannda straightened, gathered around him what was left of his dignity, and said, almost too low to hear: ''Lord of the Volcano, colleagues, clanfolk . . . I have opposed the proposal. I could possibly be mistaken. There is no mistaking that quarrels

among us . . . like this . . . are worse than anything else that might happen. Better we be destroyed by outsiders than by each other. . . . I withdraw my opposition."

He turned and stumbled toward his bench. On impulse, Yewwl picked up his harp and gave it to him.

After a hush, Wion said, not quite steadily, "If none has further speech, let the thing be done."

The inscribed parchment felt stiff in her fingers, and somehow cold.

She tucked it carefully into her travel pack, which lay by her saddle. Not far off, her tethered onsar cropped, loud in the quietness roundabout. Yewwl had wanted a while alone, to bring her whirling thoughts back groundward. Now she walked toward the camp, for they would be making Oneness.

They were out on the plain. The short, stiff nullfire that grew here glowed in the last light of the sun, a red step pyramid enormous amidst horizon mists. Lurid colors in the west gave way to blue-gray that, eastward, deepened to purple. In the north, Mount Gungnor was an uplooming of blackness; flames tinged the smoke of it, which blurred a moon. Northwestward the oncoming storm towered, flashed, and rumbled. The air was cold and getting colder. It slid sighing around Yewwl, stirring her fur.

Ahead, a fire ate scrubwood that the party had collected and waxed ever more high and more high. She heard it brawl, she began to feel its warmth. They were six who spread their vanes to soak up that radiance. The others were already homebound. Skogda, his retainer and companion Ych (oh, memory), Zh of Arachan were male; Yewwl's retainers Iyaai and Kuzhinn, and Ngaru of Raava, were female; Yewwl herself made the seventh. More were not needed. Maybe seven were too many. But they had wanted to go, from loyalty to her or from clan-honor, and she could not deny them.

Let them therefore make Oneness, and later rest a while; then she would call Banner, who would be standing by about the time that Fathermoon rose. And the ship would come — the new ship, whereof a part could hold breathable air — and carry them east at wizard speed.

Yewwl winced. She had not liked lying before the assembly. Yet she must. Else Wion would never have understood why she needed a credential which, undated as was usual, made no mention, either, of cooperation by the star-folk. After all, he would have asked, were they not star-folk too in—?—but he would have failed to remember what the place was called, Dukeston. Yewwl herself had trouble doing that, when the noise was practically impossible to utter.

She likewise had trouble comprehending that star-folk could be at strife, and in the deadly way Banner had intimated. Why? How? What did it portend? The idea was as bewildering as it was terrifying. But she must needs keep trust in her oath-sister.

Oneness would comfort, bring inner peace and the strength to go onward. Skogda had started to beat a tomtom, Kuzhinn to pipe forth a tune. Feet were beginning to move in the earliest rhythms of dance. Zh cast fragrant herbs onto the fire.

It would be an ordinary Oneness, for everybody was not perfectly familiar with everybody else. They would just lose themselves in dance, in music, in chanted words, in winds and distances, until they ceased to have names; finally the world would have no name. Afterward would be sleep, and awakening renewed. Was this remotely akin to what Banner called, in her language, "worship"? No, worship involved a supposed entity dwelling beyond the stars—

Yewwl put that question from her. It was too re-minding of the strangeness she would soon enter, not as an emissary—whatever she pretended—but as a spy. She hastened toward her folk.

IX

Clouds made night out of dusk, save again and again when lightning coursed among them. Then it was as if every huge raindrop stood forth to sight, while thunder, in that thick air, was like being under bombardment. Though the wind thrust hard, it was slow, its voice more drumroll than shriek. The rain fell almost straight down, but struck in explosive violence. Through it winged those small devil shapes that humans called storm bats.

Hooligan descended. Even using her detectors, it had not been easy, in such weather, to home on Yewwl's communicator. It might have been impossible, had Banner not supplied landmarks for radars and infrascopes to pick out. Nor was it easy to land; Flandry and the vessel's systems must work together, and he felt how sweat ran pungent over his skin after he was down.

But time was likely too short for a sigh of relief and a cigarette. He swept a searchbeam about, and found the encampment. The Ramnuans were busy striking a tent they had raised for shelter, a sturdy affair of hide stretched over poles. He swore at the delay. They'd have no use for the thing where they were bound—except, of course, to help make plausible their story that they had fared overland. He might as well have that smoke.

And talk to Banner. He keyed for her specially rigged extension. "Hello. Me. We're here," he said, hearing every word march by on little platitude feet.

"Yes, I see," came her voice from Wainwright Station. More remoteness blurred it than lay in the hundreds of kilometers between them. She was hooked into her co-experience circuit, she was with Yewwl and of Yewwl. The extension was audio only

because there would have been no point in scanning her face; she never looked away from the screen. Yet Flandry would have given much for a glimpse of her.

"Anything happen since I left?" he asked, mainly against a silence that the racket of the gale deepened.

"In those few minutes?" Did she sound irritated. "Certainly not."

"Well, you did mean to give your people a halfway plausible explanation of this sudden scurry."

"I told Huang what we'd agreed on. He may have been a bit skeptical, but I'm not sure. Now do be quiet. I've got to help Yewwl lead the rest aboard; they know nothing about spacecraft. And we're afraid the onsars will balk."

The man broke the connection, fired up the promised cigarette, and punished his lungs with it. Huang, skeptical? That could spell trouble, if and when the second in command was interviewed by ducal agents. *Why shouldn't he doubt us, though? I would*, Flandry thought. *Granted, a nasty, suspicious mind is part of my stock in trade, while he's supposed to be an unworldly scientist. Nevertheless —*

He reviewed the situation. He had nothing else to do at the moment. It would have been folly, on the order of that committed by the famous young lady named Alice, to confide in the station personnel. A few might be inclined to support him, but most would be shocked, especially the majority of Hermetians. Everybody grumbled at the slow throttling of their work; most wanted climate modification and deplored how Cairncross had dragged his tail. But it was a quantum jump from that to acceptance of possible rebellion, and to defiance of both his authority and the Emperor's. Someone would be certain to call Dukeston or Port Asmundsen and warn. Ducal militia were (supposedly!) few in this system, more a rescue corps than a police force; but it wouldn't take many to abort Flandry's mission.

Overtly, therefore, he had simply come to Ramnu to see for himself. If he decided the climate project was worthy, he would use his good offices at court. On this trip tonight, the announced plan was for him to observe native life, employing Yewwl/Banner as guide.

Everything was quite reasonable in outline. The details were the problem, as commonly with lies. Why had he waited till sunset to depart? Why had Banner gotten her fellows who also practiced linkage to urge their Ramnuans to contact Yewwl on her way to the Volcano? Explanations—that he felt he must first absorb a lot of information from the data banks; that she hoped a formal appeal by the clans would exert moral pressure on the Imperium— were inevitably weak.

Flandry had relied on the basic human tendency to swallow any positive statement. After all, these people lived insulated from politics, except for what they played among themselves; besides, to them, *he* represented Authority. But the yarn would come unraveled at the first tug on it by a professional investigator. And if Huang, or whoever, called one in, even before Cairncross' troubleshooters arrived—

Well, that wouldn't be long in any event. Meanwhile Banner sat chained to her unit. It could not be shifted aboard the spacecraft, being integral with the station. What could happen to her if she was arrested was the stuff of nightmare, sleeping and waking, for whatever excess time Flandry survived.

I've sacrificed enough lives and dreams by now, haven't I? Not hers too! Max's daughter, facing the risk with his curt gallantry and planning against it with his remembered coolness. The cigarette stub scorched his fingers. He crushed it as he would a foeman. *And she's become the closest friend I've got, maybe the only real friend, for I am certainly not one to myself.* He shivered back from any thought of love. It had never been a lucky thing to be in love with Dominic Flandry.

"The Ramnuans are prepared to board, sir," Chives reported on the intercom.

"Eh?" The man adjusted a viewscreen. Yes, there they came, leading their animals through the rain-cataract. An extruded ramp awaited them, their route into a compartment of the hold. He'd seal it off during flight.

An onsar studied the metal shape before it and grew suspicious. It dug hoofs and extensors into the ground. Its brethren took their cue from that, milled about, stamped, butted snouts at their masters, heedless of reins and thorny whips. Might they stampede?

"Beasts of burdensome," Flandry muttered in frustrated anger. They couldn't be abandoned, they were essential to the deception.

"Excuse me, sir," Chives said. "I believe if I went out I might be of assistance."

"You? In that gravity?"

"I will fly on impellers, of course."

"What's your scheme? I think nature's better equipped me for any such job."

"No, sir. You are too important. Anticipating difficulties, I have taken the liberty of donning my spacesuit, and am about to close the faceplate and cycle through. Should an accident occur, I suggest that for dinner you heat the packet numbered 'three' in the freezer. The Eastmarch Gamay Beaujolais '53 would complement it well. But I trust you will not be forced to such an extremity, sir."

"Carry on, Chives," Flandry said helplessly.

Wind made a steady roar about the hull, which

trembled under its force. Rain smote like hammers. Lightning flew, thunder rattled teeth in jaws. No matter how well outfitted, a skinny old Shalmuan aflit in that fury, in the grasp of that gravity, could well lose control and be dashed to his death. *And still he plays his part. Well, it's the sole part he can play, alone among aliens; therefore I must play mine without ever faltering. We can never really communicate, but this dance we dance between us does say, "I care for you."*

Flandry need not have worried, though. It soon became a joy to watch how elegantly Chives darted through the air. He had set his blaster to lowest beam, and the onsars had thick hides. However, the

flicks of energy suffced to herd them, and then chastise them. They shuffled aboard as meek as tax-payers.

Flandry whooped laughter. "How about that, Banner?" he cried.

Her voice was strained. "The hull screens Yewwl's signal. We're cut off. Can you relay?"

"Nothing so complex, I'm afraid."

"Well, then, get to your destination fast!" she shrilled.

Chives came back inboard. Flandry prepared to lift.

Banner spoke in a subdued tone. "I'm sorry, Dominic. I shouldn't have yelled at you. Nerves overstrung."

"Sure, I understand, dear," he said. Inwardly: *Do I? How deep into her soul does that linkage go? She can break it for a while without pain, but what if it broke forever?*

Hooligan rose, leveled off, and lined out east-northeast. She had to fly low, lest by malevolent luck a ship going to or from Port Asmundsen should notice. Despite her ample capabilities, Flandry didn't like it. He felt boxed in.

Regardless, the journey was uneventful—for him and Chives; surely not for the Ramnuans, who must be terrified in their metal cave, weighing a seventh of what they ought to, under light they saw as harsh blue-white, while cloven air rumbled and screamed outside and that which they breathed grew foul. Banner could have reassured Yewwl, but Yewwl and her followers now had naught but courage to up-hold them. A scanner showed them iron-steady. Flandry admired.

The storm fell behind. He passed fully into this planet's long, long night. Plains grew frost-silvery; snow whitened hillcrests, and not all that fell in the dark would melt when day returned. Had he lacked

optical amplification, he would have been virtually
blind. Diris was a crescent, half Luna size though
brighter; Tiglaia showed tiny; Elaveli was not aloft,
and would have seemed smaller yet. The visible
stars were few and dim, save for the red spark of
Antares, and the Milky Way was lost to sight.

Five thousand kilometers rolled beneath, and he
approached a coast. Ahead glimmered the Chromatic Hills, where Dukeston stood amidst its mines
and refineries and—what else was there. Beyond,
the St. Carl River ran down into brackish marsh-
lands, once rich with life and still, he had heard,
worth harvesting. Beyond those, an ocean lay slug-
gish until winds raised monstrous billows upon it.
In recent years, the waves had brought icebergs
crashing ashore.

They mustn't detect *Hooligan* at the settlement.

Flandry's navigational system identified a site he and Banner had chosen off maps, blocked from view by an outcrop which a few hours' riding would serve to get around. He made a gingerly descent onto roughness and told the woman, flat-voiced: "We're here."

"Good. Let them out." Her words quivered. "Send them on their way."

"A minute first, just a minute," he begged. "Listen, I can flange up an excuse for returning to Wainwright this soon. Then I'd be right there, for snatching you away if the Duke's boys come."

"No, Dominic." She spoke softer than before. "We agreed otherwise. How did you say? 'Let's not put all our eggs in one basket.'" Her chuckle was tender. "You have a marvelous gift for making phrases."

"Well, I—Look, I've been thinking further. Yes, you have to keep in touch with Yewwl till her task's accomplished, or till everything falls apart for us. And, yes, in the second case, *Hooligan* ought to remain at large, in the faint hope that something can be done some different way. But . . . you probably don't appreciate how powerfully armed she is. We can fight through anything Cairncross is likely to send, at least that he's likely to send at first. And we can outrun everything else."

Banner sighed. "Dominic, we discussed this before. You yourself admitted that that requires opening fire at the start, on little or no provocation. It gives us no flexibility, no chance to get more clues. It puts this station, its innocent staff, its work of centuries, in mortal danger. It alerts the Duke so thoroughly that his whole force will be mobilized to kill us or keep us at a distance. What can we do after that? Especially if we're wrong and he is not plotting a coup. Whereas, if he merely knows you've been skulking about—"

"He'll take what precautions he's able," Flandry

interrupted, "and the precautions that involve you won't make your future worth reaching. . . . Well, I had to ask, but I knew you'd refuse. We'll stay by the original plan."

"We're wasting time right now."

"True. Very well, I'll let the Ramnuans off, and Chives and I will go wait at the place agreed on."

Incommunicado, for fear of detection. It will be a hard wait. In several ways, harder for me than for her. She'll be in the worse peril, but she'll be with her oath-sister.

"Goodbye, darling."

X

Things have the vices of their virtues. Today Edwin Cairncross had reason to curse the fact that there was no interstellar equivalent of radio. He actually caught himself trying to imagine means of getting past the unfeasibility. The "instantaneous" pulses emitted by a ship in hyperdrive are detectable at an extreme range of about a light-year. They can be modulated to carry information. Unfortunately, within a few million kilometers quantum effects degrade the signal beyond recovery; even the simplest binary code becomes unintelligible. The number of relay stations that would be required between two stars of average separation is absurdly enormous; multiply by the factor necessary for just several hundred interconnections, and you find it would take more resources than the entire Empire contains.

But couldn't something very small, simple, cheap be devised, that we can afford in such quantities? I'll organize a research team to look into it when I am Emperor. That will also help rouse enterprise again in the human race.

Cairncross checked the thought and barked laughter. He'd have plenty to do before his throne was that secure! Until then, he should be thankful. When messages took half a month or more to go straight from Hermes to Terra, and few ships per year made the entire crossing, his realm was satisfactorily isolated. Only ambiguous hints as to what might be amiss trickled back from an undermanned Imperial legation. With patience, intelligence, sophistication, a bold leader could mount a mighty effort in obscure parts of his domain. Lacking that advantage, he could never have given flesh and steel to his desire.

Therefore, let the Empire be thankful too.

Meanwhile, though, he had no way of tracing Admiral Flandry. Where was the old devil a-prowl? The single certainty was that he had not reported in at Hermes as he was supposed to. Well, it was also known that he had left Terra, and that the Abrams bitch had disappeared under the kind of queer circumstances you'd expect him to engineer.

Cairncross hunched forward in his pilot seat. The speedster had no need of his guidance, but he felt he drew strength from the power at work below his fingers. A touch, and he could release missiles capable of wiping out a city, or the sunlike flame of a blaster cannon. He sat alone here, but within this same hull were men who adored him. Niku stood before him in heaven, become the brightest of the stars, and yonder poised nearly half the force he would presently unleash, to make himself lord of a hundred thousand worlds.

Maybe that's why I'm going in person, when I decided I'd waited too long at home on Flandry. I could have dispatched a trusty officer, but it feels good to be in action again, myself. Cairncross scowled. *Besides, he might outwit anybody else. I know better than to underestimate him.*

A waft of chill seemed to pass through the air that rustled from the ventilator. *If he went directly, he's been there for days.*

Cairncross squared his shoulders and summoned confidence. How could a solitary human creature evade his precautions in that scant a time? Nigel Broderick allowed no laxity. No stranger would get access to any place where he might see what was building. *After all, my original idea was to neutralize Flandry by bringing him to Hermes.*

Just the same —

We'll take no chances, we'll strike immediately and hard. In a few more hours, Cairncross would be on the moon Elaveli, issuing orders. Let Broderick lead a detachment to Port Lulang and occupy it, on the grounds that he was searching for a spy — true, as far as it went. But probably Flandry was on Ramnu. *I'll command the planetside operation. The stakes are too high for a lesser player. They are the destiny of civilization.*

Brief wistfulness tugged at Cairncross. He'd cherished a secondary hope of winning Flandry over to his cause. The man would be valuable. *And why shouldn't he join me? What does he owe Gerhart? He's been slighted, ignored, shunted aside. I'd have the brains to reward such a follower as he deserved, and listen to him. My aim is to give the Empire the strong, wise government it so desperately needs, to found a dynasty armored in legitimacy against usurpers . . . yes, then I'll clone myself. . . . Why, there'll no longer be any reason not to reverse the glaciation on Ramnu. In fact, it will be a suitably glorious achievement for my reign. An entire race of beings will revere my name for as long as their sun endures.*

Though that will be the littlest part of what I shall do. I could be remembered through the lifetime of the universe.

Beneath the triumphant vision went a sigh. It is very lonely to be an embodiment of fate. He had daydreamed of gaining a friend in Flandry; their spirits were much alike, and the officer's derisive humor would relieve the Emperor's austere seriousness. But as matters had developed, the odds were that Cairncross would seize the other, wring him dry of everything he knew with a deep hypnoprobing, and mercifully obliterate what was left.

Civilization was deathly ill; the rot had reached the heart. Nothing could save it but radical surgery.

Yewwl's first encounter was with a couple of native workers. Her party was riding toward Dukeston, which was as yet hidden from sight by a ridge in between. Its lights made a glow that night-adapted eyes saw as brilliant. Thence rolled a low rumbling, the sound of machines at their toil. Here the land seemed untouched. Hills lifted stark, white-

mantled save where crags reared forth, above gorges full of blackness. Frosty soil rang beneath hoofs; stones rattled; brush cracked. The air hung still and bitterly cold, making the travelers keep their vanes wrapped around them; breath formed frost crystals that lingered in glittery streamers. Overhead twinkled more stars than a human would have seen unaided, though fewer than Yewwl had observed on pictures from Terra. Mothermoon was a crescent, scarcely moved from its earlier place among them, while Fathermoon was well down the sky. Childmoon rose tiny in the east.

The strangers appeared suddenly, around the corner of a bluff. They halted, like Yewwl's group. Stares went back and forth. She saw them quite clearly, except that she couldn't be sure of the precise color of their fur. It was paler than hers, and the two were tall and slender. In their hands and strapped to their thighs they carried objects that must be made by star-folk.

After a moment, one of them spoke something that could be a question. Yewwl opened and drooped her vanes, trying to show she didn't understand. She emphasized it by saying aloud, "We share not the same language."

To her surprise, the male of the pair addressed her in Anglic. He had less vocabulary and grammar than she had acquired from Banner, and neither of them had a vocalizer to turn the sounds into those that a human would have formed. Nevertheless, a degree of comprehensibility got through: "Do you know this talk?"

"Yes," she replied.

—"Don't admit to knowing much," Banner warned in her head. "They mustn't identify you."

"A little," Yewwl added, nervously fingering the scarf that hid her collar. "How did you guess?"

"You are from afar," the male answered shrewdly.

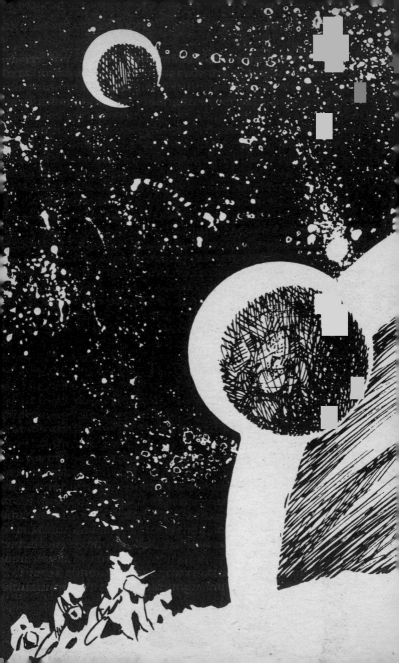

"I have never seen your kind before, though my mate and I range widely in our work. But they say that off westward is another human settlement, and I thought you might well have come from there. None of the barbarians known to us do any business here."

Communication was not truly that easy. It was full of obscurities, false starts, requests for repetition, annoyed rephrasings. But persistence kept it limping along.

Like many local natives, in these hills and the marshes below, the couple were employed by the star-folk. Live timber cruisers, harvesters, and so forth—including operators of various machines—came cheaper than robots. They were paid in trade goods, by which this region had become prosperous but upon which it was now, after centuries, totally dependent. (—"Don't you think we have been kinder to your people at Wainwright?" Banner murmured.) These two were prospectors, searching out the ores for which Dukeston's appetite had become insatiable of late. The colony itself had grown at the same pace. Why? Who knew? The humans must have their reasons, but those were beyond the grasp of simple Ramnuans.

Yewwl bristled to hear that.

She gave a brief explanation of her ostensible errand, and the pair guided her band onward. This was an exciting development for them! *En route*, she cautioned her followers anew, "Forget not: say nothing about our having been flown here, should we meet somebody who knows our tongue. We are supposed to have spent days going overland. Nor ever let fall that I am in tie with a star-person. We are to spy out what may be a hostile territory, under guise of being envoys. Let me talk for everyone."

"I seize no sense," Ngaru of Raava complained.

In truth, the idea of organized enmity was vague

and tricky as wind, and felt as icy. "Suppose a feud is between Banner and the clan-head at this place," Yewwl said. "Their retainers are naturally loyal to them, and thus likewise at odds."

"But we're asking for her/his help," Kuzhinn protested. "Why should we abide with the House of the Banner, which gives us naught?"

The time for explanation had been far too short—not that Yewwl had a great deal more to go on, herself, than faith in her oath-sister. "Banner would help us if she could, and in a mightier way," Yewwl said. "First she must overcome those who are holding her back from it. She believes the leaders here are among them. I don't expect they would ever really grant aid. Why should they? It is with the House of the Banner that the clans have ancient friendship."

"What is it, again, that we are to do?" Iyaai inquired.

Yewwl rumpled her vanes in sign of exasperation. "Whatever I tell you," she snapped. "Belike that will mainly be to stay cautious. I alone will know what to look for."

—"Will I indeed?" she asked her distant comrade.

—"*I* will, seeing through your eyes," the woman reminded her. "Don't get reckless. I could hardly bear to have anything bad happen to you . . . on my account."

—"On account of us all, I think."

Skogda clapped hand to knife. "If luck turns ill," he said, "let me take the lead. I'll make sure they know they've been in a fight!" His retainer Ych growled agreement.

"You will do what you're told, as long as I remain a-glide," Yewwl responded angrily. Inside, she wondered if her son was capable of obedience. She wished she could confide her fears to Banner. But what good would it do? Her oath-sister had woe abundant already. She could not so much as stir her body while the mission lasted. That took a bleak bravery Yewwl knew she herself lacked.

The travelers topped the ridge, and Dukeston blazed ahead. Yewwl had sufficient knowledge of such places, from what Banner had shown and explained over the years, that she was not utterly stupefied. She recognized an old central complex of buildings, akin to those at Wainwright Station. Newer, larger units spread across several kilometers of hills. She discerned housing for native workers, foreign though the designs and materials were. Elsewhere, structures that droned or purred must hold industries of different kinds. The enigmatic shapes that moved along the streets were machines. Air intake towers bespoke extensive underground installations. (Banner identified those, adding that the air was altered for her race to breathe.) A paved field some ways off, surrounded by equipment, bore a couple of objects that the woman said were moonships. Overhead circled raindrop shapes that she said were aircraft, armed for battle.

Despite this, it was mostly a dream-jumble, hard to see; the mind could not take hold of forms so outlandish. Besides, the illuminating tubes above the streets were cruelly bright. They curtained off heaven. Had she not had Banner with her in spirit, Yewwl might well have turned and fled.

As was, she must encourage her companions. Their vanes held wide, their fur on end, they were close to panic—apart from Skogda, in whom it took the form of a snarl that meant rage. The onsars were worse, and must be left in care of folk who came out to meet the newcomers. Yewwl's party continued afoot. Between these high, blank walls, she could scarcely glide had she sought to, and felt trapped.

At the end, she stopped in a square whereon were tiers of benches. It faced a large screen set inside a

clear dome.—"Yes, this is for assemblies," Banner declared in Yewwl's head. The magnified image of a man appeared.—"I've met him occasionally," Banner said. "The deputy chief, an appointee of Duke Edwin's. . . ." Yewwl did not follow the second part.

Talk scuttled back and forth until a female human was fetched to interpret. Using a vocalizer, she could somewhat speak the language of the clans; unaided Ramnuan pronunciation of Anglic seemed to baffle her. "What is your purpose?" she demanded.

Yewwl stepped forward. The blood was loud within her; both vanes throbbed to its beat. She saw in blade-edge clarity each single line, curve, hue on the face in the screen, the face that was so dreadfully like Banner's. If those lips released a particular word, she and her son and their companions would be dead.

—"Courage," came the whisper. "I know her too, Gillian Vincent, a fellow xenologist. I felt sure they'd call on her, and . . . I think we can handle her."

Yewwl took forth her parchment, which she had been holding, and unrolled it before the screen for inspection. Banner laughed dryly.—"She can't read your written language very well, but doesn't want to admit it. Quite likely she won't notice your name, if you don't say it yourself."

That had been a fang of trouble in the planning. The document was bound to specify its bearer, and her relationship to Wainwright Station was well-known. Since the name was common, and the scheme implausibly audacious, it could be hoped that no suspicions would rise. But—

"Declare your purpose," Gillian Vincent said.

Yewwl described her request for help against the Ice, the offer to exchange resources or labor for it. At first the woman said, "No, no, impossible." Prompted by Banner, Yewwl urged the case. At last the man was summoned back into view. Conference muttered.

—"I can hear them fairly well. They don't know what to make of this, and don't want to dismiss you out of hand," Banner exulted. "The bureaucratic mentality." That bit was in Anglic, and gibberish to Yewwl.

In the end, Gillian Vincent told her: "This requires further consideration. We doubt we can reach the kind of agreement you want; but we will discuss it among ourselves, and later with you again. In the meantime, we will direct our workers to provide you food and shelter."

Eagerness blazed high in Yewwl. Those folk would take for granted that newly arrived foreigners—primitives, in their viewpoint—would wander about gaping at the marvels of the town. And nobody would suppose that primitives would recognize the secret things Banner thought might be here.

Whatever those were.

XI

Hooligan flitted back westward until the broad dim sheet of Lake Roah glimmered below her. The terminator storm had moved on and the night was at peace.

There was no peace in Flandry. The lines were drawn harsh in his face and his fingers moved with controlled savagery as he piloted. The navigation system and a map found for him the bay on the south marge that Banner had picked. Instruments told him that everything was sealed; Chives pattered about to make certain. For a minute, gravity drive roiled water, then the little ship was under the surface. She sank fifty meters before coming to rest in ooze and murk.

Her topside was less far down. Flandry shut off or damped powered units as much as he could. The lake screened most emission, but not all; an intensive search could find him, and he lived by the principle of never giving an enemy a free ride. The largest demand on the generators while lying quiet was for the interior fields that maintained normal weight against Ramnu's pull. It helped to be oriented lengthwise, not needing a tensor component to keep feet drawn deckward as when the vessel was in vertical mode. Yet six out of seven standard gees were still being counteracted. He and Chives could endure being heavier than on Terra— say two gees—for as long as they must endure this wait.

First he activated one of the numerous gadgets he had had made for *Hooligan* over the years. A miniature hatch in the outer hull opened and a buoyant object emerged, trailing a wire. Its casing was of irregular shape; unless you came within centimeters, it looked like a chance bit of vegetable matter, on any of hundreds of planets, bobbing about. In reality, it was an antenna and a fish-eye video scanner. Transmitted, computer-refined, optically amplified, the image on the screen beneath was of less than homeview quality—"but 'tis enough, 'twill serve," Flandry judged. He set a monitor to sound an alarm if a member of certain classes of objects appeared. Thereafter he reduced the negagravity, and his mass laid hold of him and dragged.

"That was fun," he said to no one in particular. "Now what shall we play?"

Can't get drunk, or drugged any different way, he thought. *If and when I need to be alert, I'll receive no advance notice. Electrostim? No, the after-euphoria might fade too slowly. I need to be mean and keen. Besides, it wouldn't feel right to sit tickling my pleasure center while Banner's in peril of her life and hurting on account of her friend.*

Ha, getting moral, am I? Probably need a fresh course of antisenescents.

He rose and made his way aft, feeling every step, feeling how he must strain to hold his spine erect. In earlier days, he had shortened his hated exercises by turning up the weight before he did them; and under standard conditions, he seldom noticed himself walking—he floated. Nowadays—Well, he wasn't yet elderly, he could still pace most men twenty or thirty years his junior, but a hundred

variable cues kept him reminded that time was always gnawing, the snake at the root of Yggdrasil. Who was it had said once that youth is too precious to be wasted on the young?

Chives was in the saloon, stooped under the burden. "Sir," he reproached, "you did not warn me of this change in environment. May I ask how long it is to prevail?"

"Sure, you may, but don't expect an answer," Flandry said. "Hours, days? Sorry. You knew we'd have to lie doggo, so I assumed you'd realize this was included." With concern: "Is it too hard on you?"

"No, sir. I do fear it will adversely affect luncheon. I was planning an omelet. Under two gravities, it would get leathery. Will sandwiches be acceptable instead?"

Flandry sat down and laughed. Why not? The gods, if any, did. *I sometimes think we were created because the gods wanted to be entertained one evening by a farce—but no, that can't be. We are high comedy at least.*

The prospector who spoke some Anglic was called Ayon Oressa'ul. Folk hereabouts did not live in the large, shared territory of a clan, but on patches of land, each owned by a single family which bequeathed a common surname to its children. Ayon was evidently trusted by the chief (?) of Dukeston, for he was put in charge of the visitors. That involved a lengthy discussion on a farseer in his house, while they waited outside. He came back to them looking self-important.

"We will quarter you in my dwelling and its neighbors," he announced. His gestures included three round-walled, peak-roofed structures. Their sameness made them yet more peculiar than did their foreign style and artificial materials. Inhabit-

ants stared at the strangers but made no advances. Their postures suggested they were used to regarding all outsiders as inferior, no matter whether one among those understood human language. "You are not to leave except under escort, and always together."

Yewwl sensed a catch of Banner's breath. It brought home anew to her how cut off her band was, how precarious its grip on events. Her natural reaction was anger, an impulse to strike out. She suppressed it. Not only would it compromise her venture, but that in turn would gust her and her companions down into mortal jeopardy. She was ready to die if that would help avenge Robreng and their young ones upon the Ice; but having worked off the worst grief, she was once more finding too many splendors in the world to wish to leave it.

She smoothed her stance and asked politely, "Why? We intend no harm, we who came in search of aid."

"You might well come to harm yourselves," Ayon said. "Or you might, through ignorance, cause damage. Things strange and powerful are at work here."

Yewwl seized the chance. "We are eager to see them. Besides being curious, perhaps we will get an idea of how our country can be rescued. Please!"

"Well . . . well, I suppose that would be safe enough."

"At once, I beg you."

"What, you do not want to rest and eat first?"

"We have no sharp need of either. Also, we fear that at any moment the humans may decide to deny our plea. Then we would be sent away, no? Unless, before, we have thought of a more exact proposal to make. Please, kind male."

(The conversation was not this straightforward. Yewwl and Ayon had gained a bit more mutual fluency, talking on the way to town, but it remained awkward. She saw advantages in that, such as not having to explain precisely—and falsely—what she had to do with Wainwright Station.)

Ayon relented. He was proud of the community he served and would enjoy showing it off. "I am required to take certain things along when conducting you," he said, and went back into his house. He re-emerged with a box strapped to his left wrist, which Banner identified as a radiophone, and a larger object sheathed on his right thigh, which Yewwl recognized as a blaster. "Stay close by me and touch nothing without permission," he ordered.

—"This is less than we hoped for," she told her oath-sister. "I meant to go about freely."

—"They're showing normal caution," the woman decided. "They can't suspect your real purpose, or you'd be prisoners. We may actually manage to turn the situation to our use. The guide may well answer key questions . . . if he continues to take you for an ignorant barbarian."

"What's going on, Mother?" Skogda asked. He radiated impatience. "What's he about?"

Yewwl explained. Her son spread vanes and showed teeth. "That's an insult," he rasped.

"Calm, calm," she urged. "We *must* put our pride away here. Later, homebound, we'll track down plenty of animals and kill them."

Ayon gave them both a hard stare. Banner saw and warned:—"Body language doesn't differ much from end to end of the continent. He senses tension. Never forget, he can call armed force to him from above."

"Skogda too is anxious to start off," Yewwl assured Ayon. "Overly anxious, maybe, but we've fared a long, gruelling way for this."

He eased. "If nothing else, you will carry back tales of wonder," he replied. "Come."

They left the native quarter and followed a street that descended into a hollow between two hills. The entire bottom was occupied by a single building, blank of walls and roof. Intake towers showed that still more was underground. Stacks vented steam and smoke. In the glare of lights, vehicles trundled back and forth.

—"That is, or was, the palladium refinery; but it's incredibly enlarged." Banner's voice shook. "Ask him about it. I'll give you the questions."

—"You'd best," Yewwl said sardonically, "for I've no wisp of an idea what you're talking about."

Discourse struggled. Ayon described the ore that went in and the metal that came out. (—"Yes, palladium.") He related how the ingots were taken to the field, loaded aboard the sky-ships, and carried off. He supposed it went to the distant home of the humans. (—"There's no reason for any planet but Hermes to import it from here, and I've never heard that Hermes is using an unusual amount. . . .")

"I will show you something more interesting," Ayon offered.

The street climbed to a crest whereon stood another big building, this one with many transparent sections—which Yewwl thought of as glass—in walls and roof. Within, beneath lights less clement than the sun, a luminance like that aboard the vessel she had ridden, were rows and tiers of tanks. Plants grew there, exotically formed, intensely green.

"Here the humans raise food they can eat," Ayon said. "It isn't vital, for the ships bring in supplies, but they like to add something fresh." Banner had already informed Yewwl of this; now the latter must translate for her followers. "In late years they have added far more rooms for the purpose, underground. Many of us worked in the construction, and no few of us now work at preparing and packing

what is gathered, for shipment elsewhere." He strutted. "It must be uncommonly tasty, for the humans to want it at their home."

—"It doesn't go there," Banner observed. "Not anywhere . . . except to a military depot?"

At her prompting, Yewwl inquired, "What else do you—your folk—make for them?"

"Lumber and *iha* oil in the lowlands. Ores in the hills, though mainly those are dug by machines after persons like me have found veins. Lately we've been set searching for a different kind. And about the same time, a number of us were trained to handle machines that make clothes and armor."

"Clothes? Armor?" Yewwl and Banner exclaimed almost together.

"Yes, come and see." Ayon took a westbound street toward the outskirts of town.

"What is all this?" Skogda asked.

"Nothing," Yewwl said. She needed silence in which to think, to sort out everything that was bursting upon her.

"Oh, no, other than naught is in the air," Skogda retorted, close to fury. "See how your own vanes are stiffened. Am I an infant, that you pouch me away from truth?"

"Yes, we fared as your friends, not your onsars," Ych added.

"*You*, a friend, an equal?" Iyaai snapped, indignant on her mistress' behalf. "You're not even in her service."

"But Zh and I are your equals, Yewwl, and have our clans to answer to," Ngaru reminded. "For them, we require you share what you learn with us, your way-siblings."

—"It may be for the best." Trouble was heavy in Banner's voice. "A fuller understanding of what's afoot may make them calmer, more cooperative. You must judge, dear."

Yewwl decided. She had thin choice, anyhow. "It begins to seem these star-folk are secretly readying for an outright attack on ours," she said. "I know not why; my oath-sister has tried to make the reason clear to me, and failed. If we see that they forge the stuff of battle here, the likelihood of it heightens."

"Attack—!" Kuzhinn gasped. "All of them together, like a pack of lopers?"

Ayon halted. His hand dropped to the blaster, his vanes and ears drew back, his pupils narrowed beyond what the glare brought about. "What are you saying among each other?" he demanded. "You do not bear yourselves like peaceful people."

Yewwl had taken a lead in moots at home and assemblies on the Volcano for well-nigh twenty years. She relaxed her whole frame, signalled graciousness with her vanes, and purred, "I was translating, of course, but I fear I alarmed them. Remember, we are completely new to this kind of place. The high walls, the narrownesses between, light, noise, smells, vehicles rushing by, everything sets us on edge. Mention of armor has raised a fear that you— the local Ramnuans—may plan to oust us from our lands, against the coming of the Ice. Or if you plot no direct attack on us, you may mount one on neighboring barbarians. That could start a wave of invasions off westward, which would finally crash over our country." She spread open palms. "Ai-ah, I know well it's ridiculous. Why should you, when you already have from the humans more than what we came seeking? But it would soothe them to see what you really do make."

—"Oh, good, good!" Banner cheered.

Ayon dropped his wariness, in a slightly contemptuous manner. "Come," he invited.

Clangor, lividness, a vast sooty hall where natives controlled engines that cut, hammered, annealed, transported . . . . a warehouse where rack after rack

held what appeared to be helmets, corselets, arm-
and legpieces, and shapes more eldritch which
Banner had names for. . . . It was as if Yewwl could
feel the woman's horror.

"You see that none of this could fit any of us,"
Ayon fleered. "It is for humans. They take it
elsewhere."

—"Combat space armor; auxiliary gear; small
arms components." The Anglic words in Yewwl's
head were a terrible litany. "I suppose he's established a score of factories on out-of-the-way worlds,
none too big to be hidden or disguised—" Urgently,
in the tongue of the clans: "Find out about those
garments."

"Yes, we receive cloth and tailor it to pattern,"
was Ayon's reply to Yewwl's leading questions. "The
finished clothes are alike, except in size and orna-
ment; yes, also for humans to wear."

—"Uniforms," Banner nearly groaned. "Instead
of making a substantial, traceable investment in au-
tomated plants, he uses native hand labor where he
can, for this and the fighting equipment and—and
how much else?"

Fear walked the length of Yewwl's spine. "Oath-
sister," she asked, "have I seen enough for you?"

—"No. It's not conclusive. Learn all you can, brave
dear." Anguish freighted the tone.

"Does this prove what you have fretted over?"
Skogda breathed.

"Thus it seems," his mother answered low. "But
we need our fangs deeper in the facts, for if the thing
is true, it is frightful."

"We will take that bite," he vowed.

Ayon led them out. "We've walked far," he said. "I
grow hungry, whether or not you do. We'll return
home."

"Can we go forth again later?" Yewwl requested.
"This is such a wonder."

He rippled his vanes. "If the humans haven't dismissed you. I've no hope for your errand. What under the sky can you offer them?"

"Well, could we go back by a different route?"

Ayon conceded that, and padded rapidly from the factory. Its metal clamor dwindled behind Yewwl. She looked around her with eyes that a sense of time blowing past had widened.

The tour had gone beyond the compact part of town. New structures stood well apart, surrounded by link fences and guarded by armed Ramnuans. The street was now a road, running along a high ridge from north to south, over stony, thinly snow-covered ground. Eastward, the hill was likewise bare of anything except brush, to its foot. There a frozen river gleamed. Across a bridge, Dukeston reared and roared and glared. Westward lay only night, wild valleys, tors, canyons, cliffs, tarns. A cold wind crept out of the wastes and ruffled her pelt. The few stars she could see were as chill, and very small. Banner said they were suns, but how remote, then, how ghastly remote. . . .

Ahead, the road looped past another featureless building which air towers showed to be the cover of caverns beneath. "What is in that?" Yewwl queried, pointing.

"There they work the new ore I spoke of earlier," Ayon said.

—"Find out what it is!" Banner hissed.

Yewwl tried. The clumsiness of conversation helped mask her directness, and the rest of her party, in their unmistakable hostility, trailed her and the guide. "*Ruad'a'a*," Ayon responded finally. "I have no other word for it. The humans use ours."

—"Oh, *shit!*" Banner exploded; and: "But why would they go to that trouble? Ordinarily they use Anglic names for such things. Get him to describe it."

Yewwl made the attempt. Ayon wanted to know why she cared. She thought fast and explained that, if the Dukeston humans valued the stuff, and her homeland chanced to be supplied with it, that would be a bargaining point for her.

"Well, it's black and often powdery," Ayon said. "They get a kind of metal from it."

—"Could be pitchblende," Banner muttered in Anglic. To Yewwl: "Find out more."

Ayon could relate little else. Native labor had done only the basic construction; after that, secrecy had clamped down. He did know that large, complex apparatus had been installed, and the interior was conditioned for humans, and machines regularly collected the residue that came out and hauled it off to dump at sea, and the end product left here in sealed boxes which must be thick, perhaps lead-lined, since they were heavy for their size.

—"Fissionable? Nobody uses fission for anything important . . . except in warheads—" The incomprehensible words from afar were a chant of desperation. In Yewwl's speech, Banner said out of lips that must be stretched tight across her teeth: "It would be the final proof. But I can't think how you could learn, my sister—"

"What is this?" Skogda growled.

"Nothing," Yewwl said hastily. "He's just been describing what they make there." If her son knew that Banner thought it might be the very house of destruction—if that *was* what Banner thought—he could go wild.

"No," he denied. "You may fool everybody else, Mother, but I can read you." His fangs glistened forth, hackles lifted, ears lay back, vanes extended and shivered. "You agreed we, your companions, have the right to know what's happening."

"Well, yes, it does seem that something weird goes on, but I don't understand what," she replied with mustered calm. "I would guess we've discovered as much as we're able to. Let's stay quiet, give no alarm, till we're safe—"

Ayon stepped backward. "The young fellow stands as if he's about to attack me," he said. His own voice and posture were charged with mistrust. "The rest of your following are fight-ready too."

"No, no, they are simply excited by this experience," Yewwl insisted. A sick feeling swept through her. Ayon didn't believe. And surely it must seem peculiar to him that a group of touring foreigners were so taut.

"Perhaps," he said. "But I've served the humans through my whole life—"

And grown loyal, as I am to Banner, Yewwl realized. *And observed that in these past few years they have been working on a thing vital to them. They have not told you what, but you sense that this is true, and for their sake you are wary. No doubt it is a reason why they put us in your charge.*

"You may be harmless," Ayon continued. "Or you may be spies for a horde plotting to sack the town, or—I know not. Let the humans investigate." His blaster came forth. "Tell your friends to hold where they are," he ordered. "I am going to call for assistance. If you behave yourselves, if you really have no evil intentions, you will not be hurt."

"What does he mean?" Skogda roared.

—"Yewwl, Yewwl." Banner's tone shuddered. "Do as he says. Don't resist. It would be hopeless. Dominic and I will free you somehow—"

"He's grown suspicious, thanks to the lot of you and the fuss you've made," Yewwl told her group. "He's sending for people to take us prisoner—"

She got no chance to explain that surrender was the single sensible course. Skogda howled and sprang.

Even as he did, his mother saw upon him his astonished regret, the instant knowledge that his nerves had betrayed him. Then the blaster shot.

Its blue-white flare would have left her blinded for a while, had she seen it full on. As was, her son's body shielded her eyes from most of it. After-images danced burning; they did not hide how Skogda crashed into Ayon and the two of them went down, but Skogda was now only a carcass which had had a great hole scorched through it.

"Ee-hooa!" shrieked Yewwl, and launched herself. Ayon was struggling out from under the corpse. His left wrist brought the caller to his mouth. "Help, help," he moaned. Yewwl was upon him. Her knife struck. She felt the heaviness of the blow, the flesh giving way beneath it. She twisted the blade and saw blood spurt.

Iyaii and Kuzhinn were shaking her. "We must flee," they were saying. "Come, please come."—In

her head, Banner stopped weeping and said almost levelly, "Yes, get away fast. They have instruments which can track you by your body heat, but first they'll need to give those to people who can use them—"

Skogda is destroyed, Robreng's son and mine, Skogda whom I bore and pouched and sent off laughing for joy on his first glide and saw wedded, Skogda who gave me grandchildren to love. This thing was done in Dukeston. Aii, aii, I will give Dukeston to the wildfire, I will strew its dwellers for the carrion fowl, I am become the lightning against them. Here I am, slayers. Come and be slain!

"Yewwl, go," Banner pleaded. "If you stay, you'll die, and for nothing. *I* will punish them, Dominic and I. Your oath-sister swears it."

Almost, Yewwl obeyed. *They can take such a vengeance as the world has never seen. Let me abide until they are ready.* A few words more would have mastered the blind rage that was grief. But—

Huang flipped the main switch. The system went off line; the night at the far end of the continent blanked out; Banner stared into his face and the barren walls behind it.

"I'm sorry, Dr. Abrams," she heard, and knew in a dim way that his formality was meant to show his regret was genuine. "I know you aren't supposed to be disturbed when you're in rapport. But you did issue strict orders—"

"What?" She couldn't see him well through her tears.

"About newcomers. You were to be informed immediately, under any circumstances."

"Yes. . . ."

"Well, we've received a call. Three spacecraft of the militia will land in half an hour. The Duke himself is aboard, and requires your attendance." Anxiety: "I hope I didn't do wrong to tell him you're here, when he asked."

"I didn't tell you not to," Banner said mechanically. *How could I have?*

Huang scowled. "What's going on, anyhow? Something deucedly strange."

"You'll hear later—"

For a moment, nearly every part of Banner's being cried to be back with Yewwl. Nothing but the memory of Dominic stood between. But he had described, unsparingly, what could happen if she fell into Cairncross' hands—to her and afterward to several billion sentient beings. Yewwl, Yewwl, Yewwl was an atom among them.

Banner removed the helmet and lurched to her feet. Flandry's words against this contingency flowed of themselves. "Listen. We have an emergency situation. As you may have guessed, the admiral didn't come here just to oblige me; it was on his Grace's personal commission. I have to leave for a while—at once—alone—No, not a word! I haven't time. Tell them I'll be back shortly. His Grace will know what I mean."

All too well, he'll know. But I can be gone by then, a flying speck on a monster world.

She ran from the chamber and the bemused man. She ran from Yewwl. It was the hardest thing she had ever done. The news of her father's death had not hurt so much.

From somewhere far down inside herself, Yewwl found speech. "Go," she commanded her followers. "Scatter. Hide in the wilderness. Make your ways home." It was no fault of theirs that they had helped kill Skogda.

They saw that her fate was upon her, and departed. Air currents streamed over the hillside. They leaped from the ridge, their vanes took hold,

they planed off into darkness.

It boomed around Yewwl. A flyer was descending. She took the blaster from Ayon's slack hand, the weapon that had slain her son. Her oath-sister had let her practice with such things in the past, for sport. She grinned at the oncoming machine, into the wickedness of its guns, and sprang.

Her own vanes thrilled. Each muscle in them rejoiced to stir, tense and flex, become one with the sky and steer her in a long swoop above the world. The chill brought blood alive in them; she felt it throb and glow. Overhead burned stars.

Had the pilot seen her? She'd make sure of that. She took aim and fired. By whatever trick, when she was shooting the beam was merely bright, it did not dazzle. It raised a sharp noise and a stormy odor. When it smote, brilliance fountained.

The flyer veered. Its wake thundered around Yewwl. She rode that surge, rising higher on it. Then she was above her foe, she could glide down as if upon prey.

A hailstorm struck. She tumbled under the blows. There was no pain, she wouldn't live long enough to feel any, but she knew she had been torn open. Somehow she recovered, kept her vanes proudly bearing her, went arching toward the frozen river. The aircraft slowed, drew near, sought to give its pilot a good look at his opponent. Yewwl saw it blurrily, through waves of blindness, but she saw it, and his head within the transparent canopy. She took aim again and held the beam fast on target.

The pilot died. His aircraft spun away, hit the ice below, broke through and sank. More machines hovered close. No matter them. Yewwl spent her last strength in swerving about and aiming herself at the opened water. She would lay her bones to rest above those of the man she had slain to her wounding. Oath-sister, farewell.

XII

———————◆———————

The technician who reported at the garage, in response to Banner's intercom call, was shocked. "Donna, you can't do that!" he protested. "Going out by yourself, at night, no preparation, not even a shot of gravanol—it's suicide."

"It's necessary, and I expect to survive," she clipped. "We've no time to squander, and gravanol spends hours reaching full effect. I've just a short ways to go, on an errand that can't wait, and I'll return immediately."

"Uh, let me accompany you, at least."

"No. You're on watch. Anyway, it'd take half an hour to rig both of us. Now help me. That's an order."

The sight of his concern softened her a mite. He was a pleasant young Hermetian who had shyly mentioned to her that a girl waited at home, and after his contract here was up they'd have the stake they needed to start a business. *But . . . quite likely he was in the Cairncross Pioneers.* She retained her martinet manner.

He set his jaw and obeyed. Armor against Ramnuan conditions was more complex than a spacesuit; you could not put it on single-handed. The minutes dragged past, clocked by her pulse. She smelled her sweat and felt it creep down her skin. Never before had she imagined that making ready—undergarb, bracings, harness, outer pieces, their assembly upon her, checkoff, tests, assistance to a gravsled, connection to life support units, strap-in, more checks and tests, closure of canopy —would be torture.

After a century of heartbeats, the vehicle did at

last lift off the ferrocrete and slide silently forward. It passed among larger ones, both crawlers and flyers, most intended for remote-controlled, tele-metered use. A sled was hardly more than a flexible means for a person or two to get about for brief periods, ordinarily operating out of a mother vessel. For instance, they might want to inspect something at close range, and perhaps send the collector robot forth from its bay aft of the cockpit, to gather speci-mens or take pictures.

When Dominic suggested this plan, he didn't know how risky the passage might become for me, Banner recalled, *and I didn't tell him.* She was no longer sure that that had been wise. Not that she feared for herself; no, exertion and hazard would be over-whelmingly welcome. But if she failed to convey the information to Flandry that Yewwl had bought for the price which has no end—

The inner gate of the sally port swung back. Ban-ner steered into the lock. For a spell she was closed off, as if in a tomb; then a valve opened, she heard the air of Ramnu whistle inward, the outer gate turned, and she came forth.

The sled had no room for an interior-field generator. Seven Terran gravities laid hold on Ban-ner. It was not as bad, at first, as a crossing from spaceship to dome with no special equipment. The suit in its manifold modules supported her, gave pressure that helped against downward pooling of body fluids, gently helped her draw breath; elastic bands ran from wrists and elbows to a framework above the well-cushioned seat; safety webs em-braced; she had swallowed a couple of stimpills, which pumped strength and alertness up from her cellular reserves. Yet already she felt the brutal heaviness through and through her, even as she peered around.

The sled was not airtight; ambient pressure was

safest in so lightly built a shell. She heard every sound loudened and tonally shifted: despite hull and helmet, louder than a Ramnuan would, whose ears were not meant for Terra's thin atmosphere. The night had become quiet, but she sensed the movement of scuttering animals, the trek of wings overhead—and high, faint, rapidly increasing, the noise of ships bound downward. She was barely in time.

With the deftness of experience, she turned the sled north and kicked in the power. The wind of her passage drowned out the booming from above, and the Sol-light on the spacefield fast receded to naught. Alone in the dark, she adjusted the helmet's optics for nocturnal vision.

There was scant light to amplify, though, and she couldn't see far with any clarity. Stars glistened scattered in blackness, moons looked shrunken and lost. The Kiiong River wound as a triple belt, ebon in the middle, gray-white on the edges where freezing advanced from either bank. The forest was a shapeless murk, the veldt hoar. Ponds and rivulets lay locked into ice. And still the cold deepened, as the week-long night wore on.

She could remember when it had only been this frigid in the last few hours before dawn. Now those were often lethal. The sun would rise on entire herds which had perished and on great reaches of land where many plants would not enter the daylight half of their cycles ever again. *Yewwl, your grandchildren will see death driven back to its polar home. This I swear by my own hope for life.* If sentience did not abate the accidents of a blind universe, what meaning had sentience itself?

And yet—*Nothing seems to stand in the way of it but this secret struggle for the throne. I daresay if Cairncross became Emperor, he'd be quite willing to hear my petition—if I hadn't antagonized him—Is it too late to make amends?*

She thrust the treachery from her with her whole force. The agony of a single world could not be weighed against the ruin of scores. *The possible ruin. Dominic said Cairncross must be planning a neat, quick, precise operation. Its aftermath may not be as bad as he fears. And those other planets are mostly abstractions to me, names, something read, something seen on a show, they do not hold my people.*

But Dominic is real! came to her. *I'm pledged to him, his cause . . . am I not? I owe him much . . . how much of it done for my father's sake, how much for the abstract people, how much for the sheer game he is always playing? I'll never know. Maybe he doesn't either. He gives away nothing of his inmost self, not to anybody.*

In a chamber of her spirit that was warm and softly lit, Max Abrams knocked out his pipe, leaned back in his worn old armchair, and said to his little girl with a solemnity that smiled, "Miri, a lot of qualities are known as virtues, but most of them don't do more than please or convenience folks. Real virtue wears different faces, of course, but it doesn't come in different kinds. One way or another, what it always amounts to is loyalty."

And if we are not loyal to our few friends, what else —in these years of the Empire —have we?

Being sure why she fled, she glanced at a clock. Cairncross would have entered Wainwright Station and learned. He'd scarcely wait passive for her to do whatever she intended. He didn't know which way she'd gone, and his means for search were limited, but he would order out a hunt regardless. Flying well above the river, she was conspicuous to several sorts of instruments. It behooved her to commence evasive tactics, ground-hugging zigzags over the veldt and between its kopjes. Those were dangerous. The sled had rudimentary automation; she was the pilot, growing more weary and mind-blunted every minute. A slight error, and seventy meters per second per second of acceleration would smash her into the planet.

A laugh fluttered in her throat. She'd enjoy her flight. Or at least, while it happened she wouldn't have time for remembering.

Hour by hour, ice grew outward over the lake. Flandry contemplated a move to deeper, still-open

water before his telltale on the surface was im-
mobilized and perhaps incapacitated. Suddenly the
alarm rang, and the grindstone of his vigil exploded
into flying shards.

He had stayed in the pilot's seat as much as possible, and was there now. An image was transitting the
watch-screen, unclear but recognizable. Blas-
phemy crackled from his lips. That was a spacecraft.
Far aloft though it cruised, he identified it as a corvette: agile enough to operate in atmosphere, armed
enough to kill a larger ship or lay a city waste.

Luck had broken down—not that it hadn't been
flimsy all along. If it had lasted, then Banner would
have fared here peacefully, he'd have taken her
aboard, she'd have told him what Yewwl had or had
not observed, and on that basis they would have
decided their next action. As was, a ducal party had
arrived first. Hearing of recent events, it was in quest
of him; he could merely hope that it sought her also.
Chances were, he was safe from immediate detection. She would not be. While her vehicle was small,
the radiations of its systems weak, those were powerful and subtle instruments yonder. She'd have to
do a masterly job of skulking. *I'd not be able to.*
Ramnu is too strange to me. Is it to her?

The ship dropped slowly under the distance-
veiled horizon. If it was tracing a standard search
pattern, it would cross twice more, low and high but
keeping this spot in its field of survey. He could
make nothing but the roughest estimate of when it
would be back, forty-five minutes, give or take half
that.

Banner, where are you?

As if it had heard, a speaker brought her voice,
likewise faint and indistinct but sufficient to make
him cry out. "Dominic, I'm close by. I lay in a gully
till I figured that ship must be gone, and I'm using
minimum amplitude on the radio." Her words

rushed. "Yewwl found clues, oh, yes. Production of combat gear, uniforms, possible military rations, certainly more palladium than a civilian economy can account for, and maybe—this isn't sure— maybe a plant for fissionable isotopes. A fight broke out and I, I'm afraid she's been killed. At the same moment, three spacecraft announced they were coming in on us, with the Duke aboard. I scrambled.

"That's the basic information, Dominic. Make what you can of it. Don't risk calling me back or picking me up. I'll be all right. You be careful, dear, and get home safe."

"Like hell," he barked into the transmitter. "Hell in truth. Stay put for five minutes, then come to the shore and hover at a hundred meters. We'll work close and open the forward cargo lock. Can you steer in through that?"

"Y-yes," she stammered, "but, oh, if it lets that ship spot you—"

"Then her captain will mightily regret it," Flandry said. "Chives," he added at the intercom, "stand by for reversion to normal weight and liftoff, followed by take-on of a gravsled in the Number One hold and whatever medical attention Donna Abrams may require."

Hardly above treetop level, *Hooligan* slunk north to the Guardian Mountains. Beyond these, she found herself over a vast whiteness, the glacier, where Cairncross' men would scarcely be. Her skipper stood her on her tail and speared skyward. Stratospherically high, he retrieved navigational data and told the autopilot to make for Dukeston at an aircraft rate. Thus he would be less liable to detection; besides, he needed time with Banner.

She reclined on the saloon bench, against cushions Chives had arranged. The hands shook with which she brought a cup of tea to her mouth.

Framed in loosened brown hair, ivory pale, her countenance had thinned during the short while past; bones stood beautifully outlined and eyes smoldered copper-flame green. The view was of stars and a cloud-bright edge of Ramnu.

"How are you?" he asked.

"Better." He could barely hear. She quirked a slight smile. "I suffered no permanent damage. The stim's wearing off, I begin to feel how exhausted I am, but I can stay awake an hour or two yet."

He sat down beside her. "I'm afraid we need you for longer than that." He grimaced. "More stim, a tranquilizer, intravenous nutrients—rotten practice. You're tough, though. Later you can take a month off and recuperate. There shouldn't be any demands on you, homebound, and not too many after you've arrived."

Despite her tiredness, a quick intelligence seized on his words. "I? Just what does that mean, Dominic?"

"Nothing is predictable," he said hurriedly. "I want to minimize the stress on you, that's all. You've gotten an undue share of it, you know." He took forth his cigarette case and they both drank smoke. "But first we must have a complete account of what Yewwl found, for immediate reference and an eventual report." He laid a taper on the table. "I've already put in the background. You describe in detail what happened at Dukeston."

Her head drooped. "I don't know if I can without crying," she whispered.

He took her hand. "Cry if you want to." She did not see him wince as he remarked, "We're used to hearing that in the Corps."

At the end, he held her close, but not for long. They were too near their goal. He and Chives medicated her, and he gave her his arm to lean on while they made their way to the control cabin. Sometimes she gulped or hiccoughed, but she buckled firmly in beside him.

The strike was meteor swift. It had to be, for surely the place possessed ground defenses. *Hooligan* burst from the sky, trailing a thunderclap. Guided by Banner, who was guided by a ghost of Yewwl, Flandry aimed at the forbidden building on the hilltop. A torpedo flew ahead, set for low yield. Fire,

smoke, debris erupted from the roof. Flandry brought his vessel about and employed energy beams like scalpels, widening the hole, baring the interior. Aircraft and missiles darted toward her where she hung. She cut them down with a few sword-slashes, swung her nose high, and climbed. Walls trembled to the noise of her speed. She was out of sight in seconds.

Flandry worked a minute or two with the autopilot. *Hooligan* curved around and departed from Ramnu. The planet became a shield, emblazoned azure, argent, and sable, against the stars.

"You can rest a piece," Flandry told Banner, and left her for the laboratory. He soon emerged, starkness on his face. "Yes," he said, "the readings and pictures are plenty good; they clinch the case. That plant was producing fissionables. I don't know where those were processed for warheads, but the outer moon is a logical guess."

She considered him, where he stood tall and, now, a trifle stooped before her. The surrounding luxury of the saloon seemed as remote as a constellation. She wasn't fatigued any more, the drugs in her would not permit that, but she felt removed somehow from her body, though it was as if she heard a chill singing go along its nerves. Her mind was passionlessly clear.

"So we have the evidence?" she asked. "We can bring it to Terra for the Navy to act on?"

He stared past her. "Matters aren't that simple, I'm afraid," he replied, flat-voiced. "Cairncross will shortly have an excellent idea of the situation. He knows Gerhart can't afford to bargain with him and won't show clemency if he surrenders. Maybe he'll flee. But you've heard my supposition that, as boldly as he's moved, he's almost ready to fight. Forewarning will rule out any immediate blow at Terra, but can't stop him from mobilizing and deploying his strength before a task force can get here. He could carry on a hit-and-run campaign for years—especially if he accepts the *sub rosa* help the Merseians will be delighted to offer. He'd hope for luck in battle; and his vanity would convince him that, one by one, the worlds will rally to his standard." He nodded. "Yes, Cairncross is a warrior born. My opinion is that if he sees himself as having any kind of chance, he'll fight."

Banner glanced back at Ramnu, already dwindled enough that the screen framed its entire image. Might such a war touch it, and forever end the dream she and Yewwl had dreamed against the Ice? She knew that then she would sorrow for as long as she lived.

"What can be done?" she inquired.

Flandry grinned like a death's head. "Well," he answered, "our friend can't have many major installations, and each must be cram-full of matériel. The unexpected loss of a single one should cripple him. I've set our course for Elaveli."

XIII

Dark, cold, silent, every system turned off or throttled down to bare minimum, *Hooligan* drifted swiftly outward in a hyperbolic orbit. It would take her close to the moon, past the hemisphere opposite Port Asmundsen. The chance of her being observed was therefore slim, no matter how many were the instruments standing sentry. If a radar beam did happen to flick her, she ought to register as a bit of cosmic scrap. No natural meteoroids attended Niku, but an occasional rock must go by on its way through interstellar space; also, during centuries of human occupation, considerable junk must have accumulated around the planet.

Weightless, Flandry entered the saloon where Banner poised in midair. He caught a doorjamb to check his flight. The flashbeam in his hand picked her features out of shadow, a sculpture of strong curves and jewel-bright eyes in a sheening coif of hair. Her light sought him in turn. For a moment they were mute.

She drew breath. "It's time for action, I'm sure." Her tone was calm, but he could guess what stirred behind it. "*Now* will you tell me your plan?"

"I'm sorry to have shunted you off like this," he said. "You deserved better. But Chives and I had a fiendish lot to do on short notice. Besides, knowing you, I decided it was best to present you with a *fait accompli.*"

"A what?"

"Listen," he said, neither grimly nor jestingly— seriously. "We can't dive in and shoot up the place ahead as we could Dukeston. That's a naval base, intended for war." *Unless I've made a grisly mistake and am scheming to slaughter x many innocents.* "No single craft could get by its defenses. Moreover, you understand it's absolutely essential that we bring word to Terra. If we don't, a blow struck here won't make any final difference. Cairncross can rebuild, in the same secrecy as before. Even if we have the luck to scatter his atoms, the temptation would be very great for an officer of his to take over the dukedom and carry on the project. That could well be from idealism; they're surely dedicated men." Flandry shrugged. "Idealism has killed a lot of people throughout history."

Her gaze intensified. "What do you intend?"

"I've programmed this ship. In a few hours, she'll reactivate herself and accelerate like a scalded bat. Shortly thereafter, she'll go on hyperdrive; she can do it closer to a sun than most. She'll proceed to Sol, resume relativistic state, and beam a call for assistance, in a particular code. That'll fetch certain Corpsmen. You won't have had anything to do under way but fix your meals, rest, and recover. Nor will you have much to do at journey's end. Just tell the captain I've left a top secret record, triple-A priority. You needn't even tell him where it is in the data bank; he'll know. You'll be interrogated at length later on, but it'll be friendly, and you can expect substantial rewards." Flandry smiled. "No doubt you can get your Ramnu job included among them."

"But you won't be there," she pounced.

He nodded. "Chives and I are going to sneak our warheads in." Her lips parted. He raised a palm. "Not a word out of you, my dear. You're not qualified to do anything further hereabouts, either by training or by your current physical condition. You've done abundantly much; and you'll be needed— needed, I repeat—on Terra."

"Why can't *Hooligan* retrieve you?"

"Too risky. She's got to keep in free fall till the

base is destroyed, if it is; and afterward, whatever craft were in space will still exist, revenge-hungry. Too many unforeseeables. A computer lacks the judgment to cope with them."

She started to say something, but curbed herself.

"We'll try to make Port Lulang, on Diris," he told her.

"Do you imagine—" Again she stopped.

I read your thought, passed through him. *Spacesuit impellers can't transport us across some twenty million kilometers —alive, anyway. The odds aren't much better if we ride a missile, especially considering the radiation belt we have to traverse. Anyhow, we'd doubtless be detected by a ducal ship. Or supposing, fantastically, we did make it, the militia will be ransacking every site where Foundation personnel are, and quizzing them under narco, to make lying impossible. How could we hide?*

"It's a tadge bit dangerous, I admit," he said lightly. "But come worst to worst, well, I've had a wine cask of fun in my life, and always did hope to depart in a hellratious blaze of fireworks."

She bit her lip. Blood broke forth and drifted away in droplets that, catching diffused light, gleamed like stars.

He thrust with a foot, arrowed across to her, hooked a leg in the rail on the outer edge of the table as she had done, and let his flashbeam bob free. His hands took her by the shoulders, his gaze came to rest on hers, and he smiled.

"I apologize for not confiding in you earlier," he said. "We simply lacked the time for arguments. But you have your mission to complete. Our mission. You're Max Abrams' daughter. You won't fail."

"You trust me too much," she whispered.

"No, I suspect I don't trust you enough," he replied. "I've learned that you're quite a girl, and can dimly see what a wonderful lot more there is to you. I'd like to continue the exploration, but—" His tongue had lost its wonted smoothness. "Banner, you're a completely *decent* human being. That kind has grown mighty rare. Thank you for everything."

She could only answer him with a kiss that lingered and tasted of blood and tears.

An airlock opened. Flandry and Chives stepped forth into space.

Sharing the orbital velocity of the ship, they did

not leave her at once. The hull seemed to lie unmoving, agleam in savage sunlight. Elsewhere were the stars in their myriads, argent sweep of the Milky Way, nebulae where new suns and worlds were being born, mysterious glimmer of sister galaxies. Elaveli filled much of the scene, its lighted three-quarters a jumble of peaks, ridges, scarps, clefts, blank plains, long shadows—airless, lifeless, a stone in heaven. Ramnu was a partial disc, gone tiny but shining lovely bright blue.

A sapphire, Flandry reflected. *Yes, another stone, where a molten ball of star-stuff should by rights have been; but this one is a precious jewel, because it holds beings who are aware. I'm glad my last expedition brought me to a thing so marvelous* — irresistibly, his mouth bent upward—*so oddball.*

Chives' voice came through his earplugs: "The weapons are emerging, sir." Bulky in his suit, but his withered green countenance visible through the helmet plate, the Shalmuan flitted ahead.

Hooligan had discharged a missile on minimum impetus. The five-meter-long cylinder moved slowly off, drive tubes quiescent. Chives caught up. Behind the blunt, deadly nose, he welded a cable which secured harness for two; near the tail he fastened a tow attachment with an electrically operated release; forward again, he installed a control box which would take over guidance. Not everything had had to be made from scratch; Flandry had had a few occasions in the past to use a torpedo for an auxiliary. Banner's sled was not adaptable to that, being underpowered and intended for planetary conditions.

The man himself was equally occupied. A cargo handler had cast forth half a dozen warheads which had been removed from their carriers. The rounded cones, a meter in height, were linked by steel cords; the ensemble tumbled leisurely as it moved, like

some kind of multiple bola. But the gaucho who would cast it was after big game. Within each gray shell waited atoms that, fusing, could release up to a megaton. Flandry went among them, pushing, pulling, till he had them in the configuration he wanted. Chives steered the missile close. Together, he and the Terran prepared the warheads for towing.

The task was lengthy, complex, beset by the special perversity of objects in free fall. By the time it was done, Flandry's undergarment was wet and reeking. An ache in every muscle reminded him that he was no young man. Chives trembled till it showed on his suit.

"Squoo-hoo, what a chore!" Flandry panted. "Well, we get to rest a while, after a fashion. Come on, into the saddle, and do you know any ancient cowboy ballads?"

"No, sir, I regret I do not even know what a cowboy is," his companion replied. "However, I retain those arias from *Rigoletto* which you once desired me to learn."

"Never mind, never mind. Let's go."

Astraddle on the cylinder, held by a reinforced

safety web, the control box under his hands, Chives at his back, Flandry cast a final glance at *Hooligan*. In the course of making ready, he had wandered from her; she looked minute and lost amidst the stars. He thought of calling a farewell to Banner. But no, she couldn't break radio silence to reply, it would be cruel to her. *Luck ride with you, you good lass*, he wished, and activated the drive.

Acceleration tugged him backward, but it was mild and he could relax into his harness. A look aft assured him that the warheads were trailing in orderly wise at the ends of their separate lines. From a clasp at his waist he took a sextant. That, a telescope, and a calculator were his instruments, unless you counted the seat of his pants. He got busy.

His intention was to round the moon and make for Port Asmundsen. This would require that he fall free during the last part of the trip; grav tubes radiated when at work. It must needs be a rather exact trajectory, for at the end he'd have seconds before the defenses knew him and lashed out. Well, he'd correct it once the base hove in view, and he'd done a fair amount of eyeball-directed space maneuvering in his time. The "broomstick" you rode when playing comet polo was not totally unlike this steed. . . .

Having taken his sights, run off his computations, and adjusted his vectors, he restowed the apparatus. Chives coughed. "I beg your pardon, sir," he said. "Would you like a spot of tea?"

"Eh?"

"I brought a thermos of nice, hot tea along, sir, and recommend it. In the vernacular phrase, it bucks you up."

"W-well . . . thanks." Flandry took the proffered flask, connected its tube to the feeder valve on his helmet, put his lips to the nipple inside, and sucked. The flavor was strong and tarry.

"Lapsang Soochong, sir," Chives explained. "I know that isn't your favorite, but feared a more delicate type would be insufficiently appreciated under these circumstances."

"I suppose you're right," Flandry said. "You generally are. When you aren't, I have to submit anyway."

He hesitated. "Chives, old fellow," he got awkwardly forth, "I'm sorry, truly sorry about dragging you into this."

"Sir, my task is to be of assistance to you."

"Yes, but—You could have returned aboard after we got our lashup completed. I thought of it. But with the uncertainties—you might conceivably make the difference."

"I shall endeavor to give satisfaction, sir."

"All right, for God's dubious sake, don't make me bawl! How about a duet to pass the time? 'Laurie From Centauri', that's a fine, interminable ballad."

"I fear I do not know it, sir."

Flandry laughed. "You lie, chum. You've heard it at a hundred drunken parties, and you've got a memory like a neutron star's gravity well. You simply lack human filthiness."

"As you wish, sir," Chives sniffed. "Since you insist."

The hours went by.

Flandry spent much of them remembering. It was true what he'd told Banner, by and large he'd had a good life. His spirit had taken many terrible wounds, but had scarred them over and carried on. More hurtful, perhaps, had been its erosion, piece by piece, as he wrought evil, unleashed destruction, caused unmerited, bewildering pain, in the service of—of what? A civilization gone iniquitous in its senility, foredoomed not by divine justice but by the laws of a universe in which he could find no meaning. A Corps that was, as yet, less corrupt, but ruthless as a machine. A career that was, well, interesting, but for whose gold he had paid the Nibelung's price.

Still he declined to pity himself. He had met wild adventures, deep serenities, mystery, beauty, luxury, sport, mirth, admiration, comradeship, on world after world after world in an endlessly fascinating cosmos. He had drunk noble wines, bedded exquisite women, overcome enemies who were worth the trouble, conversed with beings who possessed wisdom—yes, except for hearth and home, he had enjoyed practically everything a man can. And . . . he had saved more lives than he ruined; he had helped win untold billions of man-years of peace; new, perhaps more hopeful civilizations would come to birth in the future, and he had been among those who guarded their womb.

Indeed, he thought, *I am grossly overprivileged. Which is how it should be.*

Port Asmundsen appeared on the limb of Elaveli. At this remove, the telescope picked out hardly more than a blur and a glitter, but Flandry got his sight and did his figuring. He made finicky adjustments on the controls. "Hang on to your bowels, Chives," he warned. "Here comes the big boost."

It was not the full acceleration of which the missile was capable. That would have killed the riders while it tore them out of their harness. But a force hauled them back for minutes, crushed ribs and flesh together, choked off all but a whistle of breath, blinded the eyes and darkened the awareness. After it ended, despite the gravanol in him, Flandry floated for a while conscious only of pain.

When he could look behind him, he saw the Shalmuan unrevived. The green head wobbled loosely in its helmet. Nothing save a dribble of blood-bubbles from nostrils showed Chives was not dead; the noise of his emergency pump, sucking away the fluid before he should choke, drowned shallow breathing.

With shaky hands, which often fumbled, Flandry took a new sight and ran a fresh computation. No further changes of trajectory seemed called for, praise fortune. To be sure, if later he found he'd been wrong about that, a burst of power at close range would give him away. But he allowed himself to hope otherwise.

There'd be little to do but hope, for the next hour or so. His velocity was high, and Elaveli would add several kilometers per second to it, which helped his chances of escaping notice. Yet he couldn't arrive too fast, for last-moment adjustments would certainly be needed and his reaction time was merely human.

"Chives," he mumbled, "wake up. Please."

Though would that be any mercy?

The death-horse plunged onward. Port Asmundsen took form in the telescope. Flandry's mind filled out the image from his recollection of pictures he had studied at Wainwright Station—

none recent. A cluster of buildings occupied a flat valley floor surrounded by mountains. Most was underground, of course. Ships crowded a sizeable spacefield. Installations were visible on several peaks, and he felt pretty sure what their nature was.

No doubt the base had a negafield generator. If his missile was identified in time, it would suddenly be confronted by a shield of force it could not penetrate, except with radiation that would do negligible damage. If it did not detonate, it would fall prey to an energy beam or a countermissile, fired from beyond the screened area. Flandry was betting that it would not be noticed soon enough.

It and its tow were just a cluster of cold bodies, smaller than the smallest spacecraft, in swift motion. A radar might register a blip, an optical pickup a flick, but the computers should dismiss these as glitches. He had hypothesized that the defenses were served chiefly by computers. Cairncross' men, especially his experienced officers, must be spread thin; he couldn't raise a substantial body of reservists until he was ready to strike, without revealing his hand. Port Asmundsen held mostly workers. (Flandry had no compunctions about them; they knew what they were working for.) Of naval personnel there, few if any could have more than a theoretical knowledge of war.

Moreover, not even a commander with battle ribbons would likely have imagined this kind of attack. Missiles were launched from warcraft, and none which didn't serve the ducal cause were known to be anywhere near. The raid on Dukeston would have brought a general alert. But the assumption was natural that *Hooligan* was bound straight home to tattle. Cairncross would have ordered a search by such vessels as had the appropriate capabilities — which meant that those vessels were not on sentry-go around Elaveli.

We'll find out, rather soon, how right I am.

Flandry felt a stirring through his harness. A weak voice trickled into his earplugs: "Sir? How are you, sir?"

"Fine and dandy," he fibbed, while his pulse throbbed relief. "You?"

"Somewhat debilitated, sir. . . . Oh, dear. I am afraid the tea flask broke free of us during acceleration."

Flandry reached to his hip. "Well," he said, "would you care to substitute a nip of cognac?"

They couldn't afford the least intoxication, but it would be best if they could relax a bit. Time was ample for regaining spryness before the last move in the game.

Presently Flandry settled himself to recalling, sight by sight, touch by touch, a girl who lay buried on a distant planet.

His attack was from the direction of the sun, whose brilliance torrented out of blackness, over knife-sharp heights and crags, across ashen valley and crouching buildings and the gaunt forms of ships. They grew below him, they reached, they reeled in his vision.

"Ya-a-ah!" he screamed, and gave a final burst of power. His thumb pushed a button. The tow attachment opened and released the warheads. They swept on. Flandry spun a pair of dials. The missile surged, the leap went through his bones, it was as if he felt the metal strain against its own speed.

"Don't look down!" he yelled. Himself he peered ahead. His groundward vector was enormous. He was fighting it with as much thrust as he could stand while remaining wholly awake, but there was no telling if he would clear the mountain before him.

Hai, what a ride! Here comes the Wild Huntsman!

The mountain was twin-peaked. With all the skill that was in him, Flandry sought the gap between. Cliffs loomed dark and sheer. Suddenly they blazed. The warheads had begun to strike.

He saw the mountain shudder and crack. A landslide went across it. Another burst of reflected lividness left him dazzled. The first flung shards hurtled incandescent around, and the first nightlike dust.

Somehow he got through. A precipice went by within centimeters, but somehow he did not crash. And he was beyond, falling toward barren hills underneath but more slowly for every furious instant. He might . . . he might yet . . . yes, by Satan, he *would* clear the horizon! He and Chives were returning starward.

When he knew that, he stared back. A pillar of murk rose and swelled, up, up, up above the shaken range. Lightnings lanced through it. That dust would quickly scatter and settle in airlessness, apart from what escaped to space. Radioactivity would poison the stone soil for years to come. The molten-bottomed craters in the valley floor would congeal around what twisted, charred fragments were left of Port Asmundsen—a terrible warning which no future powermonger would heed.

Well, but there was sufficient evidence for a properly equipped investigative team. No question survived as to what had been hatching here. Flying, Flandry had seen camouflaged portals torn open by quake and collapse; the glare of his bombs had bounced off torpedoes, artillery, armored vehicles, nothing that an honest provincial governor needed or would have concealed.

He felt incalculably glad. It would have been unbearable had his final great fireworks show destroyed harmless folk. Peace welled forth within him.

Elaveli fell behind. The residue of its former velocity, combined with the acceleration to escape, had put the missile in orbit—an eccentric orbit about Ramnu or Niku or the core of the galaxy, not yonder poor damned moon. No matter which. He'd try for Diris, but only from a sense of duty to Chives' sense of duty. With his primitive equipment, the chances of getting there before the tanked air gave out, or just of getting there, were less than slight. Besides, under drive they'd be easily detectable by any warcraft that hurried back to learn what catastrophe had happened. Whether or not the multiple blast was seen from afar, neutrino bursts had carried the news at light speed.

Flandry grinned. He kept a warhead. If an enemy tried to capture him, he'd produce one more pyrotechnic display—unless the captain was smart and opened fire immediately, which wouldn't be a bad way to go either.

He turned off the engine and let his bruised flesh savor its immemorial dream of flying weightless. Quiet laved him. The sun at his back, he saw the host of his old friends the stars.

"Sir," Chives said, "permit me to offer congratulations."

"Thank you," Flandry replied. "Permit me to offer cognac." They had no reason not to empty the flask. Rather, every reason prevailed for doing so.

"Are you hungry, sir? We have rations, albeit not up to your customary standard."

"No, not yet, Chives. Help yourself if you are. I'm quite satisfied."

Soon, however, the Shalmuan asked, "Excuse me, sir, but would it not be advisable to begin course corrections?"

Flandry shrugged. "Why not?"

He took aim at Ramnu and set off at half a gee, about as much as he guessed his companion could

take without pain. They would continue to draw
farther away for—he wasn't sure how long—until
their outward velocity had been shed. Then they
would start approaching the planet; when they got
close, he could pick out the inner moon and attempt
rendezvous. The whole effort was ridiculous . . .
except that, yes, it probably would attract a war-
ship, and death in battle was better than death by
asphyxiation.

It was bare minutes until Chives announced, "Sir, I
believe I spy a spacecraft, at six o'clock and minus
thirty degrees approximately. It seems to be nearing."

Flandry twisted about and extended his telescope. "Yes," he said. Inwardly: *If he's armed, we
fight. If he's a peaceful merchantman—I have my
blaster. Maybe when we've boarded, we can com-
mandeer him. . . . No.* The hull grew fast in his
sight. *That's no freighter, not with those lines.*

He choked on an oath.

"Sir," Chives said, audibly astounded, "I do think

it is the *Hooligan.*

"What the—the—" *I can but gibber.*

The spearhead shape glided close. Flandry halted acceleration, and his ship smoothly matched vectors. Across a few hundred meters he saw an outer airlock door swing wide. He and Chives unharnessed and flitted across.

Nobody waited to greet them when they had cycled through. Flandry heard the low throb of full power commence, felt its pulse almost subliminally. *Hooligan* was running home again. He shed his armor and shuffled forward along the corridor under a planet's weight of exhaustion. Chives trailed at a discreet distance.

Banner came from the pilot cabin. She halted amidst the metal, and he did, and for many heartbeats there was silence between them.

Finally he groaned: "How? And why, why? Compromising the mission—"

"No." Pride looked back at him. "Not really. No other vessel is in a position to intercept us. I made sure of that, and I also dispatched a written report in a message carrier, before turnabout. Did you suppose a daughter of Max Abrams would not have learned how to do such things?"

"But—Listen, the chances of our survival were so wretched, you were crazy to—"

She smiled. "I gave them a better rating. I've come to know you, Dominic. Now let's tuck you both in bed and start the therapy for radiation exposure."

But then her strength gave way. She leaned against the bulkhead, face buried in arms, and shuddered in sudden weeping. "Forgive me! I, I did wrong, I know, you must despise me, that c-c-couldn't follow orders, and me a Navy brat, but I n-n-never was any good at it—"

He gathered her to him. "Well," he said, with hardly more steadiness, "I never was either."

XIV

Fall comes early to the High Sierra. When Flandry was free of the Cairncross episode and its aftermath, that range in western North America was frosty by day and hard frozen by night. It was also at its fairest. He owned a cabin and a few hectares. Banner had stayed on Terra; first Naval Intelligence had questioned her in depth, and afterward civilian travel to planets of the Hermetian domain was suspended until security could be made certain. They had rarely communicated.

At last he could call and invite her to join him for a vacation. She accepted.

They left the cabin next morning on a hike. Chives took a fishing rod in another direction, promising trout meunière for dinner. In the beginning, man and woman walked silent. The air was diamond clear; breath smoked, and blew away on a cold breeze that smelled of fir. Those darkling trees were intermingled with golden-leaved aspen, which trembled and rustled. On the right of the trail, forest stood thin and soon came to an end. Thus wayfarers could see between trunks and boughs, to a dropoff into a canyon. On its opposite side, a kilometer distant, bluish rock lifted too steep for more than a few shrubs to grow, toward heights where snow already lay. The sky was cloudless, the sun incredibly bright. A hawk hovered, wings aglow.

After a while Banner said, looking straight before her, "We didn't talk about politics, or much of anything, yesterday."

"No, we'd better things to do, hm?"

The earnestness that he remembered was back upon her. "What is the situation? Nothing worthwhile comes in the news, ever."

"Of course not. The Imperium isn't about to publicize an affair like that. Embarrassing. And dangerous; it might generate ideas elsewhere. The fact of a conspiracy to rebel and usurp can't be totally hidden away. But it can be underplayed in the extreme, it can be made downright boring to hear about, and more entertaining events can be manufactured to crowd it out of what passes for the public consciousness."

She clenched her fists. "You know the facts, don't you?"

He nodded. "Obviously. I'm not supposed to mention them, and I wouldn't to most people, but you can keep your mouth shut. Besides, you've earned the right to learn whatever you want to."

"Well, what has happened?"

"Oh, let's not drag through the details. The whole movement fell to pieces. Some crews surrendered voluntarily, gave help to the Imperialists—led them to the various installations, for example—and have been punished by no more than dishonorable discharges, fines, or perhaps a bit of nerve-lash. Others fled, whether disappearing into the Hermetian population or establishing new identities on different planets or leaving the Empire altogether."

"Cairncross?"

"Unknown." Flandry shrugged. "I apologize for lacking a tidy answer, but life is always festooned with loose ends. It's been ascertained that his speedster was in the hunt for us when we blew his moon base out from under him. Presumably he skipped. However, interrogations of associates lead me to think the men aboard wouldn't unanimously have felt like staying under the command of an outlaw, a failure. They could have mutinied, disposed of him and the vessel, and scattered.

"No large matter, really. At worst, the Merseians or a barbarian state will gain an able, energetic

officer—who'll dwell for the rest of his years in a hell of frustration and loneliness. What counts is that he and his cause are overthrown, discredited, *kaput*. We've been spared a war.''

She turned her head to regard him. "Your doing, Dominic," she said.

He kissed her briefly. "Yours, at least as much.

You inherited your dad's talents, my dear." They went on, hand in hand.

"What about Hermes and the rest?" she asked.

Flandry sighed. "There's the messy part. Hermes did have legitimate grievances, and they still obtain. I talked the Emperor into leniency for the people — no purges or mass confiscations or anything like that. He and the Policy Board do want changes which'll take away what extra power Hermes had. Its authority everywhere outside the Maian System has been revoked, for instance, and it's under martial law itself, pending 'reconstruction.' But you can't blame Gerhart too much; and, as said, ordinary people are being allowed to continue their ordinary lives. They're good stock; they'll become important again in the Empire . . . and afterward."

Her gaze held wonder. "The Emperor heeds you?"

"Oh, my, yes. We maintain our mutual dislike, but he realizes how useful I can be. And for my part, well, my advice isn't the worst he could get; and his son and heir isn't such a bad young fellow. I'm afraid I'll end my days as a kind of gray eminence." He paused. "Though scarcely in holy orders."

"I'll get you to explain that later," she said. Her voice stumbled. "What about Ramnu?"

"Why, you do know that the climate modification project has been approved, don't you?"

"Yes." Barely to be heard: "Yewwl's memorial. Her name will be on it."

"Work can't start till things have gotten satisfactorily organized in that sector. A couple of years hence, I'd guess. Thereafter, maybe a decade till completion, and three or four more decades till the glaciated territory has been reclaimed, right? But the Ramnuans will get assistance meanwhile, I promise."

"Thank you," she breathed. Tiny brightnesses

glinted on her lashes, around the big green eyes.
"The interdict on travel ought to be lifted soon.
Are you eager to return?"

"I could be helpful."

Flandry stroked his mustache. "You haven't exactly answered my question. Tell me, if you will—You didn't need to hang around on Terra this entire while. You could have gone to your family on Dayan."

"Yes, I should have."

"But you didn't. Why?"

She stopped, and he did, and they stood facing in the nave made by trail and trees. A yellow leaf blew down and settled in her hair. He took both her hands. They were cool.

She spoke with a resolution she must have been long in gathering: "I had to think. To understand. Everything has changed, been shattered, could be rebuilt but never in the same shape. Half of me died when Yewwl did. I need new life, and came to see—it was slow, finding the truth, because the search hurt so much—I don't want to begin again with another Ramnuan. Our sisterhood, Yewwl's and mine, was wonderful, I'll always warm my soul by it, but it came to be when we were young, and *that* is gone."

The forest soughed. Wind boomed through the canyon. "I stayed on Terra, Dominic, because of hoping you and I would meet again."

"I spent the whole time hoping I'd hear those words," he replied.

When the kiss had ended, he said to her: "Let's be honest with each other, always. We're not a boy and girl in love. We're both a little old, more than a little sad, and friends. But we make one crackling hell of a team. A pity if we disbanded. Would you like to continue?"

"I think I would," she told him. "I certainly want to try. Thank you, dear friend."

They walked on into the autumn.

Afterword:
The Price of Buying Time

by
Sandra Miesel

We have watched Dominic Flandry selling his soul piece by piece to earn a reprieve for the doomed Terran Empire. Why were these sacrifices necessary? What did they accomplish? Answering these questions requires an historical survey of Technic civilization.

A thousand years before Flandry's time, the woeful twentieth century faded into the hopeful twenty-first. Widespread social upheaval triggered by war, famine, and other disasters had obliterated entire societies but the ultimate effect was to produce a freer international order. Rational solutions were found to old problems like energy and population. The emerging global society was firmly wedded to technology and largely—but by no means exclusively—Western in outlook. Although local tongues persisted, the universal language was Anglic, a simplified version of English enriched with many foreign loan words. The new cultural synthesis became known as Technic civilization, successor of Western as Western had been of Classical.

The prosperity of this new era provided the resources to explore and develop the Solar System. Colonies were placed in orbit and permanent bases were established on the Moon and planets. A less-than-successful attempt was made to terraform Venus. By 2100, these settlements were large enough to join Earth in establishing the Solar Commonwealth, an institution that was to endure for the next five centuries. At the same time, faster-than-light interstellar travel became possible. Exploration and then emigration proceeded with explosive vigor. ("Wings of Victory" and "The Problem of Pain" occur in this period.)

Colonies continued to be founded all during the Commonwealth age. Just like New World pioneers before them, colonists were drawn by the chance for adventure, profit, advancement, social and political experimentation, or the desire to preserve a unique cultural heritage. (The ethnic motive was paramount for the settlers of Russo-Mongol Altai, African Nyanza, and Slavic Dennitza, to name only a few examples.) This outflow of humanity to widely scattered independent worlds is known as the Breakup.

Furthermore, humans encountered numerous other intelligent races among the stars. Contact was generally peaceful and mutually beneficial. (Mars was ceded to aliens suited to its environment, a precedent for the later cession of Jupiter to the Ymirites in Imperial times.) Many alien peoples could assimilate high technology and interact with men as equals. All had contributions to offer: arts, beliefs, information, goods, services, and so forth. These exotic stimuli sparked the creative energies of Technic civilization to new peaks of excellence because they broadened the range of options available to each individual.

Thus interstellar conditions in Commonwealth times approximated those of the European Age of Exploration during the sixteenth and seventeenth centuries. Likewise, they bred the same boldness. Independent traders ranged across vast reaches of space discovering and exploiting new worlds. Daring merchant-adventurers amassed huge fortunes and enormous political power. Their resources surpassed those of whole planetary governments, enabling them to live as grandly and arrogantly as feudal princes.

In the twenty-third century, the merchants and other groups involved in trade formed the Polesotechnic League to foster their own interests. This "League of

Selling Skill" was a voluntary, self-regulating mutual protection organization that sought to curb the worst excesses of unbridled capitalism and defend its members against outside foes such as governments. The League issued its own currency, conducted its own diplomacy, and, on occasion, raised its own armies. Overall, it resembled the Hanseatic League of mercantile cities which totally dominated northern European commerce and politics between the thirteenth and fifteenth centuries.

But the League made fateful decisions at a meeting called the Council of Hiawatha in 2400 which turned it into a set of feuding cartels and left it open to Commonwealth interference. The inability of the League to discipline itself and maintain its independence doomed it in the same way as the Conciliarist Movement's failure to reform the Church had doomed medieval Catholicism a thousand years before.

Nevertheless, the League's sunset years were filled with glorious accomplishments as exemplified in the careers of flamboyant Nicholas van Rijn and his soberer protégé David Falkayn. Stories featuring these men (see accompanying chart) illustrate the positive effects of the League on human colonists and primitive aliens. The traders imparted useful knowledge, reconciled warring factions, thwarted outside aggressors, loosened internal repression, suppressed piracy, and brought new groups into interstellar society—earning profits all the while. With van Rijn's consent, Falkayn helped underdeveloped planets acquire essential capital which proved to be their margin of survival later on. Together they exposed schemes of subversion and conquest that threatened Earth herself (*Satan's World* and *Mirkheim*).

But the League had irreparably decayed by the end of van Rijn's lifetime because of its members' greed and ruthlessness and the overwhelming complexity of its operations. By then, the Commonwealth had become a weak but meddlesome bureaucracy whose fortunes were intertwined with the League's. Falkayn, who had married van Rijn's granddaughter, foresaw the end and eventually emigrated from Technic civilization's sphere. He founded the new colony of Avalon which was jointly populated by humans and the winged Ythrians and ruled by the Domain of Ythri. ("Wingless on Avalon" and "Rescue on Avalon" relate the early years of this important settlement.)

Falkayn retreated; others built barricades against the coming storms. The next two centuries were the Time of Troubles. Technic civilization was swept by continual waves of war, revolution, economic collapse, and all their attendant evils. Violent convulsions shook every society—some fatally. The nadir was the sack of Earth by the Baldic League, a pack of spacegoing barbarians who had acquired advanced weapons from irresponsible traders. Shortly afterwards, the alien Gorzuni began raiding Earth periodically for slaves to stock their budding empire. One of their captives, Manuel Argos, organized a successful slave revolt that began the liberation of Earth ("The Star Plunderer"). Argos was a charismatic—and pragmatic—leader of enormous energy. Once he had stabilized the ravaged Solar System, he proclaimed himself First Emperor of the Terran Empire. This was a symbolic title shrewdly calculated to appeal to exhausted beings' longing for order.

Stability was what the Empire promised; stability was what it delivered. Other systems and regions willingly united with Terra in order to enjoy her protection. The Empire's rule was mild and the benefits of security from attack, safe transportation, and easy communication were immense. Terra collected only modest taxes for the support of her excellent Navy and Civil Service and generally let member planets manage their internal affairs undisturbed.

This was the ideal which attracted the allegiance of sturdy old colonies like Dennitza. Although some worlds, such as Aeneas and Ansa, had to be annexed forcibly, their inhabitants soon recognized the value of provincial status. "Sargasso of Lost Starships" is an account filled with discrepancies, nevertheless it shows the early Empire defeudalizing stagnant Ansa to good effect.

The turning point in Terra's expansion was the costly war of aggression that she fought against the Domain of Ythri. "Rectification of borders" was the official excuse; the true motive was sheer territorial aggrandizement. Although some Ythrian planets were won, bicultural Avalon successfully resisted Terran conquest as related in *The People of the Wind*. Eventually the Empire grew to encompass a sphere 400 light years in diameter, englobing four million stars and 100,000 inhabited planets. Now its only desire was to preserve that dominion unmolested.

Although both the Commonwealth and the Empire were created after periods of universal chaos, note that a century of redevelopment had preceded the formation of the Commonwealth whereas the Empire sprang directly from the ruins of previous institutions. This difference in origins produced considerable divergence in operation and attitudes. The Commonwealth as a political entity never extended beyond the Solar System, yet its era was a time of new accomplishments, broad horizons, and healthy cross-cultural influences. Men's attention was focussed outward on other worlds, other races. Colonies were scattered broadcast and the Polesotechnic League harvested trade across incredible distances.

The Empire, on the other hand, was founded for renewal rather than development. Terra's task was to restore and preserve Technic civilization, hence her citizens were often cautious, incurious, and reluctant to try anything really new. There was even a lack of initiative in adapting to conditions on other worlds (Llynathawr, Freehold). Technology, especially for military purposes, did advance but basic scientific research lagged. The arts were likewise stagnant, chiefly repeating ancient models. Terrans were now less responsive to alien influences than formerly although colonials like the Dennitzans continued cultural interactions with their resident aliens. Overall, the Empire's outlook was parochial and protective whereas the League's had been ecumenical and expansionist.

After two centuries, these negative traits had become cracks fissuring the Empire's structure. But although Terra and her most imitative subjects were crumbling, the weaknesses in the foundation did not necessarily touch alien complexes within the Empire or colonies with strong, indigenous cultures of their own. (The cleavage between urban and rural Freeholders in "Outpost of Empire" is a case in point.) Nevertheless, the sound and unsound parts of the Empire were in jeopardy together.

The once-efficient system of Emperor and executive Policy Board acting through Sector Governors and planetary Residents was breaking down under the weight of personal corruption and folly. The Imperial yoke grew heavier without any offsetting increases in benefits, making the provinces resentful. More and more often, Terra's rulers were either too short-sighted to recognize threats to the public welfare or too stingy to meet them. One contemporary civil servant said of the Empire:" 'Its competent people become untrustworthy from their very competence; anyone who can make a decision may make one the Imperium does not like. Incompetence grows with the growing suspiciousness and centralization. Defense and civil functions alike begin to disintegrate. What can that provoke except rebellion?' " (A Knight of Ghosts and Shadows).

Unlike the working aristocrats on colonial worlds such as Aeneas, the Terran upper classes were largely composed of selfish parasites exploiting their position for private gain. Titles of nobility ceased to be rewards for excellence as society hardened into castes. Options dwindled for the lower classes. Slavery was revived as punishment for crime. Indifference to aliens cost opportunities for wonder and sometimes masked a casual racism. The position of women declined in practice if not in theory. Vigorous colonial women and female aliens continued the Commonwealth-era tradition of full participation in society but too many Terran women were simply menials, consorts, entertainers, or whores. (Compare with the difference in feminine roles in nineteenth century frontier America and contemporary Second Empire France.)

Detachment, boredom, apathy, despair were the prevailing moods of the era. Terrans lost their confidence, their morale, their energy. As one observer remarked: " 'We've given up seeking perfection and glory; we've learned that they're chimerical—but that knowledge is a kind of death within us,' " ("Honorable Enemies"). The world-weary sought consolation in vice or spiritual obsessions. Few even thought of resisting the Empire's inevitable fall. A nineteenth century historian's verdict on Byzantium is equally applicable to the Terran Empire: "It is a tale of what had reached its zenith, of what was past its best strength, a tale of decadence postponed with skill and energy, and yet only postponed."

Matters were far otherwise with Terra's fierce young rival, the Roidhunate of Merseia. This newer imperium would never have come into existence except for David Falkayn's intervention when Merseia was threatened by the effects of a nearby supernova ("Day of Burning"). But the League's high-handed relief tactics outraged the haughty Merseians so thoroughly, they were spurred to achieve global union. In due course, they entered space and emerged from the Time of Troubles ruling an interstellar empire composed of many peoples, including humans. However, since this was the Merseians' first turn on the wheel of galactic history, they were as energetic and ambitious as Earthmen of the early Commonwealth period had been.

Merseia's collision with Terra was another example of that old adage: "Two tough, smart races want the same real estate." Despite their green reptilian skins, Merseians were enough like humans to eat the same food and enjoy the same jokes. However, they were more ferocious than humans and could tolerate no equals whatsoever. To them, the Covenant of Alfzar they signed with Terra was no treaty of detente but an invitation to continue their struggle by covert means.

A Merseian conceived of life as a great hunt and found the meaning of his existence in the strength of the foes he overcame. The bellicose Merseians relished interspecies struggle but would not have hesitated to exterminate vanquished opponents afterwards. They were proud and severe by nature but the Roidhunate's acute xenophobia was a feature of the dominant, Eriau-speaking culture, not necessarily of their entire people.

Merseian allegiance was primarily to the race, not to the Roidhunate as such. Their ultimate goal was nothing less than a Merseian-owned galaxy. Their governing Grand Council of Vachs (clan chiefs) headed by a landless, hereditary head of state (the Roidhun) had no direct aspirations to direct galactic rule but rather envisioned interlocking sets of autonomous Merseian realms. They believed their great vision justified any policy, however ruthless.

Although the warfare between Terra and Merseia resembles innumerable matches between weary old empires and brash new ones, the closest historical analogy is to the Eastern Roman Empire's duel with Sassanid Persia between the third and seventh centuries A.D. Both pairings were instances of disastrous, mutually exhausting struggles between enemies who regarded each other as their sole worthy opponent. The Eastern Empire was as preservationist, inward-turning, callous, and sophisticated as the Terran. It was perennially on the defensive against waves of enemies both civilized and barbarous. Key factors in its survival were devious intelligence agents and military officers who were hedonists in the capital but heroes in the marches.

The Sassanids, on the other hand, were an aggressive, chauvinistic dynasty supremely confident of Persian cultural superiority. The intolerant state religion they ardently patronized justified their pretentions. Their obsession with hunting and their fiercely romantic masculinity were uncannily Merseian in flavor.

Terran-Merseian rivalry had smoldered for about a century when Dominic Flandry was born in the year 3000. He was the bastard son of a scholarly minor nobleman and an opera singer. Flandry had a keen mind in an agile body, a gift for languages, a ready wit, a flair for showmanship, and dazzling personal charm. He was part cynic, part idealist, self-indulgent and dedicated by turns, a refined voluptuary forever trying to explain away his good deeds. His sanguine-melancholic personality made him resilient, adventurous, and romantic to the point of sentimentality. Although descended from many racial stocks (a black ancestor appears in *The People of the Wind*), Flandry best fit the "Gallic" ethnic stereotype. He characterized himself as a "spoiled gentleman," explaining: " 'Personally I enjoy decadence; but somebody has to hold off the Long Night for my own lifetime, and it looks as though I'm elected,' " ("Hunters of the Sky Cave").

But Flandry's predominant fault, the one that caused the most grief for himself and others, was his total inability to understand women. He called them "the aliens among us" and no matter how passionately or how frivolously he pursued them, he never grasped their nature. The women who loved him—and there were many—suffered cruelly on his account. This is a common enough pattern for a rake who had been neglected by his mother, but in Flandry's case it had grave historical consequences.

Brilliant feats of improvisation marked Flandry's career as a Naval Intelligence officer. Of course not all his accomplishments have been chronicled, but the following were significant. (See the chart for detailed chronology.) He saved the two intelligent native races of Starkad and the Terran Navy from destruction in *Ensign Flandry*. But in order to achieve this, he callously exploited a courtesan's devotion and thus sowed the seed of future personal tragedy. ("Flandry knew in full what it meant to make an implement of a sentient being.") His first espionage venture cost him the freshness of his youth.

In *A Circus of Hells*, Flandry uncovered a Merseian spy network and foiled its plot to detach an entire Sector from the Empire. Through his efforts the planet Talwin became a neutral scientific base jointly operated by Merseia and Terra. Once more he reached his objective over a woman's body, this time with even less awareness of wrong-doing than in *Ensign Flandry*. But this outraged mistress, a poor prostitute, was psychically gifted. She cursed him never to possess the woman he loved most.

Within a few years he met and lost his great love in *The Rebel Worlds*. She was Kathryn McCormac, the wife of an admiral driven into revolt against the Empire by an Imperial Governor's brutal exactions. With Flandry's help she killed the Governor, thus preventing him from becoming the future evil power behind the Imperial throne. But she permitted her husband's rebellion to fail and followed him into exile rather than commit adultery with Flandry, whose disappointment became an excuse for libertine living.

Although this threat to the Empire's integrity was successfully countered, the ominous precedent of military revolt had been set. In the future it would be copied by other Navy officers hopeful of becoming "barracks emperors." Aeneas, focal point of the rebellion, was subsequently pacified and reconstructed despite Merseian attempts to reopen the wound (*The Day of Their Return*).

Later Flandry singlehandedly ruined the invasion plans of the barbarian Scothani and brought them under Imperial rule after seducing and manipulating their young queen ("Tiger by the Tail"). For this victory he was knighted. In "Honorable Enemies," he preserved the neutrality of Betelgeuse by deceiving Merseia's top intelligence agent, the phenomenal non-Merseian telepath Aycharaych. Simultaneously, Flandry rejected the love of a Terran noblewoman without recognizing the unselfishness of her attitudes. This episode opened years of a bitter—and bitterly regretted—vendetta between Flandry and Aycharaych. Two years later in "The Game of Glory" Flandry detected and killed a Merseian secret agent on the water world Nyanza. This time he rebuffed the attention of a beautiful woman for motives that approached chivalry.

On the steppes of Altai Flandry frustrated Merseian plans to annex that planet. This adventure ("A Message in Secret") was mercifully free from psychological torment. Then on the way home, Flandry liberated the hermit world of Unan Besar from a fiendish, biochemically based tyranny but afterwards deserted the loyal whore who had made his success possible ("A Plague of Masters").

In "Hunters of the Sky Cave" Flandry tore apart another of Aycharaych's webs by helping expel alien invaders, the wolf-like Ardazirho, from the human colony Vixen. Once the aggressors were turned into allies, the Empire used their fleet to crush the Merseians at the Battle of Syrax. The poignance of this episode was not so much in Flandry's sentimental dalliance with a Vixenite girl but in his warmer rapport with aliens than Imperials.

The Syrax victory not only averted military peril, it made such a hero of participating Terran Admiral Hans Molitor that his troops soon proclaimed him Emperor after the reigning Josip died childless. This dynastic crisis took three years to settle. Meanwhile, Flandry gained fame by rescuing the favorite granddaughter of one elderly interim Emperor from the harem of a treacherous Duke with Imperial ambitions of his own in "The Warriors from Nowhere." Later, Flandry worked closely with Molitor during the consolidation of his reign and thus became a trusted personal advisor to him and his dynasty.

All the strands of Flandry's past knotted together in *A Knight of Ghosts and Shadows.* He foiled simultaneous plots to fan racial tensions and to goad the valuable planet Dennitza into rebellion against the Empire. Flandry was about to marry Kossara, a Dennitzan aristocrat who resembled his lost Kathryn, but the fruit of his youthful sins destroyed his last chance for happiness. His own son by his first mistress turned traitor, brought about his fiancee's death, and was killed at his order afterwards. Behind all the shadows stood Flandry's old antagonist Aycharaych. Flandry discovered and destroyed Aycharaych's home world, a vacant storehouse of ancient wisdom. This revenged Kossara and cost the Merseian Intelligence Service a priceless resource.

Drained but still effective, Flandry eventually achieved a peace of exhaustion in his private life by settling down with Miriam Abrams, daughter of the officer who had originally led him into intelligence work. He and Miriam destroyed a would-be Hitler of Argolid descent on Hermes (*A Stone in Heaven*). Flandry ended his days as the gray eminence behind Hans Molitor's grandson.

Besides extending the lifespan of the Empire by at least a century, Flandry's deeds had important longer range consequences. The natives of Starkad, Talwin and Ramnu survived to pursue their own promising destinies. The Scothani and Ardazirho were brought into the orbit of Technic civilization and tamed somewhat. New opportunities were opened for humans on Altai and Unan Besar. Some of the McCormac rebels may have become the ancestors of the intrepid Kirkasanters in "Starfog." Vixen developed itself well enough to found a daughter colony, New Vixen, that later became a major center of civilization. Aeneas and Dennitza remained so strong they outlived the Empire and helped re-establish order in their Sectors. Most importantly, every one of the myriad lives Flandry saved was another ripple in the pool of time.

But Flandry was only manning the pump on a sinking ship. The Empire could stay afloat a while longer but it was no longer able to repair—much less rebuild—itself. Destructive trends continued in Terran society despite the sacrifices of Flandry and others like him: "Too many mutually alien races; too many forces clashing in space, and so desperately few who comprehended the situation and tried their feeble best to help—naked hands battering at an avalanche as it ground down on them," ("Honorable Enemies").

Creativity never revived in the arts and sciences. Social barriers grew higher and the gaps between classes wider. Slaves increased in numbers while the conditions of their servitude worsened. Terra's fear of colonial disloyalty grew after McCormac's Revolt but her countermeasures, like forbidding Navy men to serve in their home systems, only weakened loyalty further. Colonies such as Freehold, Aeneas, and Dennitza began to plan for their post-Imperial futures. Despairing of Technic civilization, ripe for new religions and crazes, people withdrew from Terran society psychologically if not physically.

Thus it was with the Terran Empire as it had been with the Roman nearly 3,000 years before. Not enough is known about the Terran Emperor Georgios to compare him directly with the Roman Marcus Aurelius but at least he was an acceptable ruler. His son Josip, however, was every bit as degenerate as Marcus Aurelius' son Commodus and his impact on the Empire every bit as disastrous. The disorders that followed Josip's death tossed up Hans Molitor who was an exact counterpart to Septimus Severus, similarly provided with two incompetent sons, and likewise destined to die on an unruly frontier. After another round of civil wars, Flandry became the key advisor to a sound, Aurelian-like Emperor.

The Terran Empire was completing its Principate phase and beginning its Interregnum in Flandry's day. After his death, it became a Dominate, a static, repressive state with all the harshness of Diocletian's Rome. All the negative tendencies of the previous era persisted unchecked. Not even a resort to divine kingship could save the Empire. The Fall, so slow, so long expected, was complete by the middle of the fourth millenium. Technic civilization was extinct. The Long Night had arrived.

Information about the Empire's Fall is inexact and largely speculative but the Byzantine-Persian historical model described earlier can usefully supplement the Roman one. It appears that Terra and Merseia wore each other out in fruitless wars of attrition, leaving each other too weak to resist other foes. Internal rebellions triggered by poverty, tyranny, and insecurity left both imperia even more vulnerable.

There may have been some new crusading movement comparable to Islam which attracted subject peoples on both sides. (Aycharaych had tried to kindle such on Aeneas and Diomedes.) Perhaps the Betelgeusans, a race noted for long range planning, had decided to end their centuries of neutrality and prosper at their larger neighbors' expense just as the medieval Georgians had. Possibly the fierce Gorrazani (descendants of the Gorzuni) erupted in conquest like the Turks. Or else the precedents of the Scothani and Ardazirho inspired other barbarians to harry Terra and Merseia as border savages had raided Byzantine and Persian territory. Undoubtedly, these were the kinds of factors that ruined Terra and Merseia. It is not certain if either capital world was destroyed. But shorn of her possessions, heavily populated Terra had insufficient resources left to rebuild her might. Merseia would have suffered catastrophic culture shock when her glorious dream failed.

A few incidents recorded during the Long Night show old Imperial colonies trying to retain or regain lost knowledge ("A Tragedy of Errors"). It was hunger for knowledge more than for goods that stimulated civilization's revival. Leading planets in the reconstruction period like Nuevoamerica and Kraken had never been part of the Empire. They explored far beyond its old borders (*The Night Face* and "The Sharing of Flesh"). Eventually, an entirely new approach to interstellar relations evolved. This was the Commonalty, a galactic service organization that provided quasi-governmental services without itself actually being a government ("Starfog"). Hopefully, the Commonalty will avoid some of the weaknesses inherent in empires but eventually it is sure to develop special problems of its own. Meanwhile, a new and brilliant cycle of history has begun.

What does the pageant of Technic civilization just summarized prove? (If indeed history can be said to *prove* anything.) First, its rise and fall demonstrates that governments operate under the social equivalent of Darwinian pressure: they must function within their environments or be replaced. Any kind of system that provides its citizens with an acceptable balance of opportunity and security is good. Pragmatic results count for more than political dogma. Initially the League emphasized opportunity and the Commonwealth security but finally neither could give either and so they perished. The best justification for the early Empire was that it spread a military umbrella over 100,000 unique cultural experiments. Once its ability to stimulate and defend its subjects faltered, its days were numbered.

Furthermore, these extant accounts of Technic civilization show history as a record of interlocking ironies arising from individual choices. For instance, if Falkayn had not aided Merseia, it would not have survived to menace the Empire. Yet if he had not also founded Avalon and his descendants not resisted Imperial conquest, no free Avalonian would have been available to save the Empire from a subtle Merseian plot in *The Day of Their Return*. If Flandry had treated his first two mistresses with greater consideration, he would not have lost his last chance for happiness. If Kathryn had not rebuffed Flandry's advances, neither the Empire nor her own descendants would have long survived. Each irresistible historic trend is actually the net product of separate acts which had not necessarily appeared significant at the time they occurred. Each key event " 'is the flower on a plant whose seed went into the ground long before . . . and whose roots reach widely, and will send up fresh growths,' " (*A Knight of Ghosts and Shadows*).

Finally, this temporal drama reminds us that everything in the universe is mortal. All things, institutions as well as persons, are born only to die. The lifespan of a galaxy or an empire is as limited as that of a man. The only proper response, in the face of entropy's inevitable triumph is to struggle as well and bravely as possible. As Flandry said in *A Handful of Stars*, " 'I don't want to die so fast I can't feel it. I want to see death coming, and make the stupid thing fight for every centimeter of me.' " Existence is a pattern with no ultimate transcendent goal, no purpose other than to be itself, a doomed but lovely candle in the darkness.

A Chronology of
Technic Civilization

Note: Although Poul Anderson was consulted during the preparation of this chart, he is not responsible for its dating nor in any way specifically committed to it. Stories are listed by their most recently published titles. Rounded dates are quite approximate.

21st C	century of recovery
22nd C	intersteller exploration, the Breakup, formation of the Commonwealth, planting of early colonies including Hermes.
2150	"Wings of Victory," *Analog Science Fiction* (cited as ASF), April, 1972. Ythri discovered. discovery of Merseia
23rd C	establishment of the Polesotechnic League colonization of Aeneas and Altai
24th C	"The Problem of Pain," *Fantasy and Science Fiction* (cited as F & SF), February, 1973.
2376	Nicholas van Rijn born colonization of Vixen
2400	Council of Hiawatha colonization of Dennitza
2406	David Falkayn born
2415	"Margin of Profit," ASF, September, 1956. (van Rijn) "How to Be Ethnic in One Easy Lesson," in *Future Quest*, ed. Roger Elwood, Avon Books, 1974.

27th C	the Time of Troubles "The Star Plunderer," *Planet Stories* (cited as PS), September, 1952.
28th C	foundation of the Terran Empire, Principate phase begins colonization of Unan Bator "Sargasso of Lost Starships," PS, January, 1952.
29th C	*The People of the Wind*. New American Library from ASF February-April, 1973.
30th C	The Covenant of Alfzar
3000	Dominic Flandry born
3019	*Ensign Flandry*. Chilton, 1966. Abridged version in *Amazing* (cited as *Amz*), October, 1966.
3021	*A Circus of Hells*. New American Library, 1970. Incorporates "The White King's War," *Galaxy* (cited as *Gal*), October, 1969. Flandry is a Lieutenant (j.g.).
3022	Josip succeeds Georgios as Emperor.
3025	*The Rebel Worlds*. New American Library, 1969. Flandry is a Lt. Commander then promoted to Commander.
3027	"Outpost of Empire," *Gal*, December, 1967. (non-Flandry)
3028	*The Day of Their Return*. Doubleday, 1973. (non-Flandry)
3032	"Tiger by the Tail," PS, January, 1951. Flandry is a Captain.
3033	"Honorable Enemies," *Future Combined with Science Fiction Stories*, May, 1951.
3035	"The Game of Glory," *Venture*, March, 1958. Flandry has been knighted.
3037	"A Message in Secret," as *Mayday Orbit*. Ace Books, 1961 from a shorter version, "A Message in Secret," *Fantastic*, December, 1959.

3038	"A Plague of Masters," as *Earthman, Go Home*. Ace Books, 1961 from "A Plague of Masters," *Fantastic*, December, 1960-January, 1961.
3040	"Hunters of the Sky Cave," as *We Claim These Stars!* Ace Books, 1959 from abridged version, "A Handful of Stars," *Amz*, June, 1959.
3041	Interregnum: Josip dies, after three years of civil war Hans Molitor rules as sole Emperor.
3042	"The Warriors from Nowhere," as "The Ambassadors of Flesh," PS, Summer, 1954.
3047	*A Knight of Ghosts and Shadows*. New American Library, 1975 from *Gal*, September/October-November/December, 1974.
3054	Hans Molitor dies, succeeded by Dietrich then Gerhart.
3061	*A Stone in Heaven*. Ace Books, 1979. Flandry is a Vice Admiral. Dominate phase
early 4th millenium	Fall of the Terran Empire
mid-4th millenium	The Long Night
3600	"A Tragedy of Errors," *Gal*, February, 1968.
3900	*The Night Face*. Ace Books, 1978 as *Let the Spacemen Beware!* Ace Books, 1963 from shorter version "A Twelvemonth and a Day," *Fantastic Universe*, January, 1960.
4000	"The Sharing of Flesh," *Gal*, December, 1968.
7100	"Starfog," ASF, August, 1967.